THE COLOSSUS
OF YLOURGNE

AND THREE OTHERS

THE COLOSSUS OF YLOURGNE

AND THREE OTHERS

CLARK ASHTON SMITH

WILDSIDE PRESS

THE COLOSSUS OF YLOURGNE
AND THREE OTHERS

"The Abominations of Yondo" was originally published in *Overland Monthly*, Vol. 84, No. 4, (April, 1926). "The Chain of Aforgomon" was originally published in *Weird Tales*, Dec. 1935. "The Charnel God" was originally published in *Weird Tales*, March 1934. "The Colossus of Ylourgne" was originally published in *Weird Tales*, June 1934.

CONTENTS

THE ABOMINATIONS OF YONDO

The sand of the desert of Yondo is not as the sand of other deserts; for Yondo lies nearest of all to the world's rim; and strange winds, blowing from a pit no astronomer may hope to fathom, have sown its ruinous fields with the gray dust of corroding planets, the black ashes of extinguished suns. The dark, orblike mountains which rise from its wrinkled and pitted plain are not all its own, for some are fallen asteroids half buried in that abysmal sand. Things have crept in from nether space, whose incursion is forbid by the gods of all proper and well-ordered lands; but there are no such gods in Yondo, where live the hoary genii of stars abolished and decrepit demons left homeless by the destruction of antiquated hells.

It was noon of a vernal day when I came forth from that interminable cactus-forest in which the Inquisitors of Ong had left me, and saw at my feet the gray beginnings of Yondo. I repeat, it was noon of a vernal day; but in that fantastic wood I had found no token or memory of a spring; and the swollen, fulvous, dying and half rotten growths through which I had pushed my way, were like no other cacti, but bore shapes of abomination scarcely to be described. The very air was heavy with stagnant odors of decay; and leprous lichens mottled the black soil and russet vegetation with increasing frequency. Pale-green vipers lifted their heads from prostrate cactus-boles and watched me with eyes of bright ochre that had no lids or pupils. These things had disquieted me for hours past; and I did not like the monstrous fungi, with hueless stems and nodding heads of poisonous mauve, which grew from the sodden lips of fetid tarns; and the sinister ripples spreading and fading on the yellow water at my approach were not reassuring to one whose nerves were still taut from unmentionable tortures. Then, when even the blotched and sickly cacti became more sparse and stunted, and rills of ashen sand crept in among them, I began to suspect how great was the hatred my heresy had aroused in the priests of Ong and to guess the ultimate malignancy of their vengeance.

I will not detail the indiscretions which had led me, a careless stranger from far-off lands, into the power of those dreadful magicians and mysteriarchs who serve the lion-headed Ong. These indiscretions, and the particulars of my arrest, are painful to remember; and least of all do I like to remember the racks of dragon-gut strewn with powdered adamant, on which men are stretched naked; or that unlit room with six-inch windows near the sill, where bloated corpse worms crawled in by hundreds from a neighboring catacomb. Sufficient to say that, after expending the resources of their frightful fantasy, my inquisitors had borne me blindfolded on camel-back for incomputable hours, to leave me at morning twilight in that sinister forest. I was free, they told me, to go whither I would; and in token of the clemency of Ong, they gave me a loaf of coarse bread and a leathern bottle of rank water by way of provision. It was at noon of the same day that I came to the desert of Yondo.

So far, I had not thought of turning back, for all the horror of those rotting cacti, or the evil things that dwelt among them. Now, I paused knowing the abominable legend of the land to which I had come; for Yondo is a place where few have ventured wittingly and of their own accord. Fewer still have returned — babbling of unknown horrors and strange treasure; and the life-long palsy which shakes their withered limbs, together with the mad gleam in their starting eyes beneath whitened brows and lashes, is not an incentive for others to follow. So it was that I hesitated on the verge of those ashen sands, and felt the tremor of a new fear in my wrenched vitals. It was dreadful to go on, and dreadful to go back, for I felt sure that the priests had made provision against the latter contingency. So after a little I went forward, singing at each step in loathly softness, and followed by certain long-legged insects that I had met among the cacti. These insects were the color of a week-old corpse and were as large as tarantulas; but when I turned and trod upon the foremost, a mephitic stench arose that was more nauseous even than their color. So, for the nonce, I ignored them as much as possible.

Indeed, such things were minor horrors in my predicament. Before me, under a huge sun of sickly scarlet, Yondo reached interminable as the land of a hashish-dream against the black heavens. Far-off, on the utmost rim, were those orblike mountains of which I have told; but in between were awful blanks of gray desolation, and low, treeless hills like the backs of half buried monsters. Struggling on, I saw great pits where meteors had sunk from sight; and divers-colored jewels that I could not name glared or glistened from the dust. There were fallen cypresses that rotted by crumbling mausoleums, on whose lichen blotted marble fat chameleons crept with royal pearls in their mouths. Hidden by the low ridges, were cities of which no stela remained unbroken — immense and immemorial cities lapsing shard by shard, atom by atom, to feed infinities of desolation. I dragged my torture-weakened limbs over vast rubbish-heaps that had once been mighty temples; and fallen gods frowned in rotting pasammite or leered in riven porphyry at my feet. Over all was an evil silence, broken only by the satanic laughter of hyenas, and the rustling of adders in thickets of dead thorn or antique gardens given to the perishing nettle and fumitory.

Topping one of the many moundlike ridges, I saw the waters of a weird lake, unfathomably dark and green as malachite, and set with bars of profulgent salt. These waters lay far beneath me in a cuplike hollow; but almost at my feet on the wave-worn slopes were heaps of that ancient salt; and I knew that the lake was only the bitter and ebbing dregs of some former sea. Climbing down, I came to the dark waters, and began to lave my hands; but there was a sharp and corrosive sting in that immemorial brine, and I desisted quickly preferring the desert dust that had wrapped me about like a slow shroud. Here I decided to rest for a little; and hunger forced me to consume part of the meager and mocking fare with which I had been provided by the priests. It was my intention to push on if my strength would allow and reach the lands that lie to the north of Yondo. Theses lands are desolate, indeed, but their desolation is of a more usual than that of Yondo; and certain tribes of nomads have been known to visit them occasionally. If fortune favored me, I might fall in with one of these tribes.

The scant fare revived me, and, for the first time in weeks of which I had lost all reckoning, I heard the whisper of a faint hope. The corpse-colored insects had long since ceased to follow me; and so far despite the eeriness of the sepulchral silence and the mounded dust of timeless ruin, I had met nothing half so horrible as those insects. I began to think that the terrors of Yondo were somewhat exaggerated. It was then that I heard a diabolic chuckle on the hillside above me. The sound began with a sharp abruptness that startled me beyond all reason, and continued endlessly, never varying its single note, like the mirth of an idiotic demon. I turned, and saw the mouth of a dark cave fanged with green stalactites, which I had not perceived before. The sound appeared to come from within this cave.

With a fearful intentness I stared at the black opening. The chuckle grew louder, but for awhile I could see nothing. At last I caught a whitish glimmer in the darkness; then, with all the rapidity of nightmare, a monstrous Thing emerged. It had a pale, hairless, egg-shaped body, large as that of a gravid she-goat; and this body was mounted on nine long wavering legs with many flanges, like the legs of some enormous spider. The creature ran past me to the water's edge; and I saw that there were no eyes in its oddly sloping face; but two knifelike ears rose high above its head, and a thin, wrinkled snout hung down across its mouth, whose flabby lips, parted in that eternal chuckle, revealed rows of bats' teeth. It drank acidly of the bitter lake then, with thirst satisfied, it turned and seemed to sense my presence, for the wrinkled snout rose and pointed toward me, sniffing audibly. Whether the creature would have fled, or whether it meant to attack me, I do not know; for I could bear the sight no longer but ran with trembling limbs amid the massive boulders and great bars of salt along the lakeshore.

Utterly breathless I stopped at last, and saw that I was not pursued, I sat down, still trembling, in the shadow of a boulder. But I was to find little respite, for now began the second of those bizarre adventures which forced me to believe all the mad legends I had heard. More startling even than that diabolic chuckle was the scream that rose at my very elbow from the salt-compounded sand — the scream of a woman possessed by some atrocious agony, or helpless in the grip of devils. Turning, I beheld a veritable Venus, naked in a white perfection that could fear no scrutiny, but immersed to her navel in the sand. Her terror-widened eyes implored me and her lotus hands reached out with beseeching gesture. I sprang to her side — and touched a marble statue, whose carven lids were drooped in some enigmatic dream of dead cycles, and whose hands were buried with the lost loveliness of hips and thighs. Again I fled, shaken with a new fear; and again I heard the scream of a woman's agony. But this time I did not turn to see the imploring eyes and hands.

Up the long slope to the north of that accursed lake stumbling over boulders of basanite and ledges that were sharp with verdigris-covered metals; floundering in pits of salt, on terraces wrought by the receding tide in ancient aeons. I fled as a man flies from dream to baleful dream of some cacodemoniacal night. At whiles there was a cold whisper in my ear, which did not come from the wind of my flight; and looking back as I reached one of the upper terraces, I perceived a singular shadow that ran pace by pace with my own. This shadow was not the shadow of man nor ape nor any known beast; the head was too grotesquely elongated, the squat body too gibbous ; and I was unable to determine whether the shadow possessed five legs, or whether what appeared to be the fifth was merely a tail.

Terror lent me new strength, and I had reached the hilltop when I dared to look back again. But still the fantastic shadow kept pace by pace with mine; and now I caught a curious and utterly sickening odor, foul as the odor of bats who have hung in a charnel-house amid the mold of corruption. I ran for leagues, while the red sun slanted above the asteroidal mountains to the west; and the weird shadow lengthened with mine but kept always at the same distance behind me.

An hour before sunset I came to a circle of small pillars that rose miraculously unbroken amid ruins that were like a vast pile of pot-sherds. As I passed among these pillars I heard a whimper, like the whimper of some fierce animal, between rage and fear, and saw that the shadow had not followed me within the circle. I stopped and waited, conjecturing at once that I had found a sanctuary my unwelcome familiar would not dare to enter; and in this the action of the shadow confirmed me, the Thing hesitated, then ran about the circle of columns pausing often between them; and, whim-pering all the while, at last went away and disappeared in the desert toward the setting sun.

For a full half hour I did not dare to move; then, the imminence of night, with all its probabilities of fresh terror, urged me to push on as far as I could to the north. For I was now in the very heart of Yondo where demons or phantoms might dwell who would not respect the sanctuary of the unbroken columns. Now, as I toiled on, the sunlight altered strangely; for the red orb nearing the mounded horizon, sank and smouldered in a belt of miasmal haze, where floating dust from all the shattered fanes and necropoli of Yondo was mixed with evil vapors coiling skyward from black enormous gulfs lying beyond the utmost rim of the world. In that light, the entire waste, the rounded mountains, the serpentine hills, the lost cities, were drenched with phantasmal and darkening scarlet.

Then, out of the north, where shadows mustered, there came a curious figure C a tall man fully caparisoned in chainmail — or, rather, what I assumed to be a man. As the figure approached me, clanking dismally at each step on the sharded ground, I saw that its armor was of brass mottled with verdigris; and a casque of the same metal furnished with coiling horns and a serrate comb, rose high above its head. I say its head, for the sunset was darkening, and I could not see clearly at any distance; but when the apparition came abreast, I perceived that there was no face beneath the brows of the bizarre helmet whose empty edges were outlined for a moment against the smouldering light. Then the figure passed on, still clank-ing dismally and vanished.

But on its heels ere the sunset faded, there came a second appa-rition, striding with incredible strides and halting when it loomed almost upon me in the red twilight — the monstrous mummy of some ancient king still crowned with untarnished gold but turning to my gaze a visage that more than time or the worm had wasted. Broken swathings flapped about the skeleton legs, and above the crown that was set with sapphires and orange rubies, a black something swayed and nodded horribly; but, for an instant, I did not dream what it was. Then, in its middle, two oblique and scarlet eyes opened and glowed like hellish coals, and two ophidian fangs glittered in an apelike mouth. A squat, furless, shapeless head on a neck of disproportionate extent leaned unspeakably down and whispered in the mummy 's ear. Then, with one stride, the titanic lich took half the distance between us, and from out the folds of the tattered sere-cloth a gaunt arm arose, and fleshless, taloned fingers laden with glowering gems, reached out and fumbled for my throat . . .

Back, back through aeons of madness and dread, in a prone, precipitate flight I ran from those fumbling fingers that hung always on the dusk behind me, back, back forever, unthinking, unhesitating, to all the abominations I had left; back in the thickening twilight toward the nameless and sharded ruins, the haunted lake, the forest of evil cacti, and the cruel and cynical inquisitors of Ong who waited my return.

THE DARK EIDOLON

Thasaidon, lord of seven hells
Wherein the single Serpent dwells,
With volumes drawn from pit to pit
Through fire and darkness infinite —
Thasaidon, sun of nether skies,
Thine ancient evil never dies,
For aye thy somber fulgors flame
On sunken worlds that have no name,
Man's heart enthrones thee, still supreme,
Though the false sorcerers blaspheme.
— The Song of Xeethra

On Zothique, the last continent on Earth, the sun no longer shone with the whiteness of its prime, but was dim and tarnished as if with a vapor of blood. New stars without number had declared themselves in the heavens, and the shadows of the infinite had fallen closer. And out of the shadows, the older gods had returned to man: the gods forgotten since Hyperborea, since Mu and Poseidonis, bearing other names but the same attributes. And the elder demons had also returned, battening on the fumes of evil sacrifice, and fostering again the primordial sorceries.

Many were the necromancers and magicians of Zothique, and the infamy and marvel of their doings were legended everywhere in the latter days. But among them all there was none greater than Namirrha, who imposed his black yoke on the cities of Xylac, and later, in a proud delirium, deemed himself the veritable peer of Thasaidon, lord of Evil.

Namirrha had built his abode in Ummaos, the chief town of Xylac, to which he came from the desert realm of Tasuun with the dark renown of his thaumaturgies like a cloud of desert storm behind him. And no man knew that in coming to Ummaos he returned to the city of his birth; for all deemed him a native of Tasuun. Indeed, none could have dreamt that the great sorcerer was one with the beggar-boy Narthos, an orphan of questionable parentage, who had begged his daily bread in the streets and bazaars of Ummaos. Wretchedly had he lived, alone and despised; and a hatred of the cruel, opulent city grew in his heart like a smothered flame that feeds in secret, biding the time when it shall become a conflagration consuming all things.

Bitterer always, through his boyhood and early youth, was the spleen and rancor of Narthos toward men. And one day the prince Zotulla, a boy but little older than he, riding a restive palfrey, came upon him in the square before the imperial palace; and Narthos implored an alms. But Zotulla, scorning his plea, rode arrogantly forward, spurring the palfrey; and Narthos was ridden down and trampled under its hooves. And afterward, nigh to death from the trampling, he lay senseless for many hours, while the people passed him by unheeding. And at last, regaining his senses, he dragged himself to his hovel; but he limped a little thereafter all his days, and the mark of one hoof remained like a brand on his body, fading never. Later, he left Ummaos, and was forgotten quickly by its people. Going southward into Tasuun, he lost his way in the great desert, and was near to perishing. But finally he came to a small oasis, where dwelt the wizard Ouphaloc, a hermit who preferred the company of honest jackals and hyenas to that of men. And Ouphaloc, seeing the great craft and evil in the starveling boy, gave succor to Narthos and sheltered him. He dwelt for years with Ouphaloc, becoming the wizard's pupil and the heir of his demon-wrested lore. Strange things he learned in that hermitage, being fed on fruits and grain that had sprung not from the watered earth, and wine that was not the juice of terrene grapes. And like Ouphaloc, he became a master in devildom and drove his own bond with the archfiend Thasaidon. When Ouphaloc died, he took the name of Namirrha, and went forth as a mighty sorcerer among the wandering peoples and the deep-buried mummies of Tasuun. But never could he forget the miseries of his boyhood in Ummaos and the wrong he had endured from Zotulla; and year by year he spun over in his thoughts the black web of revenge. And his fame grew ever darker and vaster, and men feared him in remote lands beyond Tasuun. With bated whispers they spoke of his deeds in the cities of Yoros, and in Zul-Bha-Shair, the abode of the ghoulish deity Mordiggian. And long before the coming of Namirrha himself, the people of Ummaos knew him as a fabled scourge that was direr than simoom or pestilence.

Now, in the years that followed the going-forth of the boy Narthos from Ummaos, Pithaim, the father of Prince Zotulla, was slain by the sting of a small adder that had crept into his bed for warmth on an autumn night. Some said that the adder had been purveyed by Zotulla, but this was a thing that no man could verily affirm. After the death of Pithaim, Zotulla, being his only son, was emperor of Xylac, and ruled evilly from his throne in Ummaos. Indolent he was, and tyrannic, and full of strange luxuries and cruelties; but the people, who were also evil, acclaimed him in his turpitude. So he prospered, and the lords of Hell and Heaven smote him not. And the red suns and ashen moons went westward over Xylac, falling into that seldom-voyaged sea, which, if the mariners' tales were true, poured evermore like a swiftening river past the infamous isle of Naat, and fell in a worldwide cataract upon nether space from the far, sheer edge of Earth.

Grosser still he grew, and his sins were as overswollen fruits that ripen above a deep abyss. But the winds of time blew softly; and the fruits fell not. And Zotulla laughed amid his fools and his eunuchs and his lemans; and the tale of his luxuries was borne afar, and was told by dim outland peoples, as a twin marvel with the bruited necromancies of Namirrha.

It came to pass, in the year of the Hyena, and the month of the star Canicule, that a great feast was given by Zotulla to the inhabitants of Ummaos. Meats that had been cooked in exotic spices from Sotar, isle of the east, were spread everywhere; and the ardent wines of Yoros and Xylac, filled as with subterranean fires, were poured inexhaustibly from huge urns for all. The wines awoke a furious mirth and a royal madness; and afterward they brought a slumber no less profound than the Lethe of the tomb. And one by one, as they drank, the revellers fell down in the streets, the houses and gardens, as if a plague had struck them; and Zotulla slept in his banquet-hall of gold and ebony, with his odalisques and chamberlains about him. So, in all Ummaos, there was no man or woman wakeful at the hour when Sirius began to fall toward the west.

Thus it was that none saw or heard the coming of Namirrha. But awakening heavily in the latter forenoon, the emperor Zotulla heard a confused babble, a troublous clamor of voices from such of his eunuchs and women as had awakened before him. Inquiring the cause, he was told that a strange prodigy had occurred during the night; but, being still bemused with wine and slumber, he comprehended little enough of its nature, till his favorite concubine, Obexah, led him to the eastern portico of the palace, from which he could behold the marvel with his own eyes.

Now the palace stood alone at the center of Ummaos, and to the north, west and south, for wide intervals of distance, there stretched the imperial gardens, full of superbly arching palms and loftily spiring fountains. But to eastward was a broad open area, used as a sort of common, between the palace and the mansions of high optimates. And in this space, which had lain wholly vacant at eve, a building towered colossal and lordly beneath the full-risen sun, with domes like monstrous fungi of stone that had come up in the night. And the domes, rearing level with those of Zotulla, were builded of death-white marble; and the huge façade, with multi-columned porticoes and deep balconies, was wrought in alternate zones of night-black onyx and porphyry hued as with dragons' blood. And Zotulla swore lewdly, calling with hoarse blasphemies on the gods and devils of Xylac; and great was his dumfoundment, deeming the marvel a work of wizardry. The women gathered about him, crying out with shrill cries of awe and terror; and more and more of his courtiers, awakening, came to swell the hub-bub; and the fat castradoes diddered in their cloth-of-gold like immense black jellies in golden basins. But Zotulla, mindful of his dominion as emperor of all Xylac, strove to conceal his own trepidation, saying:

"Now who is this that has presumed to enter Ummaos like a jackal in the dark, and has made his impious den in proximity and counterview of my palace? Go forth, and inquire the miscreant's name; but ere you go, instruct the headsman to make sharp his double-handed sword."

Then, fearing the emperor's wrath if they tarried, certain of the chamberlains went forth unwillingly and approached the portals of the strange edifice. It seemed that the portals were deserted till they drew near, and then, on the threshold, there appeared a titanic skeleton, taller than any man of earth; and it strode forward to meet them with ell-long strides. The skeleton was swathed in a loin-cloth of scarlet silk with a buckle of jet, and it wore a black turban, starred with diamonds, whose topmost foldings nearly touched the high lintel. Eyes like flickering marsh-fires burned in its deep eye-sockets; and a blackened tongue like that of a long-dead man protruded between its teeth; but otherwise it was clean of flesh, and the bones glittered whitely in the sun as it came onward.

The chamberlains were mute before it, and there was no sound except the golden creaking of their girdles, the shrill rustling of their silks, as they shook and trembled. And the foot-bones of the skeleton clicked sharply on the pavement of black onyx as it paused; and the putrefying tongue began to quiver between its teeth; and it uttered these words in an unctuous, nauseous voice:

"Return, and tell the emperor Zotulla that Namirrha, seer and magician, has come to dwell beside him."

Hearing the skeleton speak as if it had been a living man, and hearing the dread name of Namirrha as men hear the tocsin of doom in some fallen city, the chamberlains could stand before it no longer, and they fled with ungainly swiftness and bore the message to Zotulla.

Now, learning who it was that had come to neighbor with him

in Ummaos, the emperor's wrath died out like a feeble and blustering flame on which the wind of darkness had blown; and the vinous purple of his cheeks was mottled with a strange pallor; and he said nothing, but his lips mumbled loosely as if in prayer or malediction. And the news of Namirrha's coming passed like the flight of evil night-birds through all the palace and throughout the city, leaving a noisome terror that abode in Ummaos thereafter till the end. For Namirrha, through the black renown of his thaumaturgies and the frightful entities who served him, had become a power that no secular sovereign dared dispute; and men feared him everywhere, even as they feared the gigantic, shadowy lords of Hell and of outer space. And in Ummaos, people said that he had come on the desert wind from Tasuun with his underlings, even as the pestilence comes, and had reared his house in an hour with the aid of devils beside Zotulla's palace. And they said that the foundations of the house were laid on the adamantine cope of Hell; and in its floors were pits at whose bottom burned the nether fires, or stars could be seen as they passed under in lowermost night. And the followers of Namirrha were the dead of strange kingdoms, the demons of sky and earth and the abyss, and mad, impious, hybrid things that the sorcerer himself created from forbidden unions.

Men shunned the neighborhood of his lordly house; and in the palace of Zotulla few cared to approach the windows and balconies that gave thereon; and the emperor himself spoke not of Namirrha, pretending to ignore the intruder; and the women of the harem babbled evermore with an evil gossip concerning Namirrha and his concubines. But the sorcerer himself was not beheld by the people of that city, though some believed that he walked forth at will, clad with invisibility. His servitors were likewise not seen; but a howling as of the damned was sometimes heard to issue from his portals; and sometimes there came a strange cachinnation, as if some adamantine image had laughed aloud; and sometimes there was a chuckling like the sound of shattered ice in a frozen hell. Dim shadows moved in the porticoes when there was neither sunlight nor lamp to cast them; and red, eery lights appeared and vanished in the windows at eve, like a blinking of demoniac eyes. And slowly the ember-colored suns went over Xylac, and were quenched in far seas; and the ashy moons were blackened as they fell nightly toward the hidden gulf. Then, seeing that the wizard had wrought no open evil, and that none had endured palpable harm from his presence, the people took heart; and Zotulla drank deeply, and feasted in oblivious luxury as before; and dark Thasaidon, prince of all turpitudes, was the true but never-acknowledged lord of Xylac.

And in time the men of Ummaos bragged a little of Namirrha and his dread thaumaturgies, even as they had boasted of the purple sins of Zotulla.

But Namirrha, still unbeheld by living men and living women, sat in the inner walls of that house which his devils had reared for him, and spun over and over in his thoughts the black web of revenge. And the wrong done by Zotulla to Narthos in old times was the least of those cruelties which the emperor had forgotten.

Now, when the fears of Zotulla were somewhat lulled, and his women gossiped less often of the neighboring wizard, there occurred a new wonder and a fresh terror. For, sitting one eve at his banquet-table with his courtiers about him, the emperor heard a noise as of myriad iron-shod hooves that came trampling through the palace gardens. And the courtiers also heard the sound, and were startled amid their mounting drunkenness; and the emperor was angered, and he sent certain of his guards to examine into the cause of the trampling. But peering forth upon the moon-bright lawns and parterres, the guards beheld no visible shape, though the loud sounds of trampling still went to and fro. It seemed as if a rout of wild stallions passed and re-passed before the façade of the palace with tumultuous gallopings and capricoles. And a fear came upon the guards as they looked and listened; and they dared not venture forth, but returned to Zotulla. And the emperor himself grew sober when he heard their tale; and he went forth with high blusterings to view the prodigy. And all night the unseen hooves rang out sonorously on the pavement of onyx, and ran with deep thuddings over the grasses and flowers. The palm-fronds waved on the windless air as if parted by racing steeds; and visibly the tall-stemmed lilies and broad-petaled exotic blossoms were trodden under. And rage and terror nested together in Zotulla's heart as he stood in a balcony above the garden, hearing the spectral tumult, and beholding the harm done to his rarest flower-beds. The women, the courtiers and eunuchs cowered behind him, and there was no slumber for any occupant of the palace; but toward dawn the clamor of hooves departed, going toward Namirrha's house.

When the dawn was full-grown above Ummaos, the emperor walked forth with his guards about him, and saw that the crushed grasses and broken-down stems were blackened as if by fire where the hooves had fallen. Plainly were the marks imprinted, like the tracks of a great company of horses, in all the lawns and parterres; but they ceased at the verge of the gardens. And though everyone believed that the visitation had come from Namirrha, there was no proof of this in the grounds that fronted the sorcerer's abode; for here the turf was untrodden.

"A pox upon Namirrha, if he has done this!" cried Zotulla. "For what harm have I ever done him? Verily, I shall set my heel on the dog's neck; and the torture-wheel shall serve him even as these horses from Hell have served my blood-red lilies of Sotar and my vein-colored irises of Naat and my orchids from Uccastrog which were purple as the bruises of love. Yea, though he stand the viceroy of Thasaidon above Earth, and overlord of ten thousand devils, my wheel shall break him, and fires shall heat the wheel white-hot in its turning, till he withers black as the seared blossoms." Thus did Zotulla make his brag; but he issued no orders for the execution of his threat; and no man stirred from the palace towards Namirrha's house. And from the portals of the wizard none came forth; or if any came there was no visible sign or sound.

So the day went over, and the night rose, bringing later a moon that was slightly darkened at the rim. And the night was silent; and Zotulla, sitting long at the banquet-table, drained his wine-cup often and wrathfully, muttering new threats against Namirrha. And the night wore on, and it seemed that the visitation would not be repeated. But at midnight, lying in his chamber with Obexah, and fathom-deep in his slumber from the wine, Zotulla was awakened by a monstrous clangor of hooves that raced and capered in the palace porticoes and in the long balconies. All night the hooves thundered back and forth, echoing awfully in the vaulted stone, while Zotulla and Obexah, listening, huddled close amid their cushions and coverlets; and all the occupants of the palace, wakeful and fearful, heard the noise but stirred not from their chambers. A little before dawn the hooves departed suddenly; and afterward, by day, their marks were found found on the marble flags of the porches and balconies; and the marks were countless, deep-graven, and black as if branded there by flame.

Like mottled marble were the emperor's cheeks when he saw the hoof-printed floors; and terror stayed with him henceforth, following him to the depths of his inebriety, since he knew not where the haunting would cease. His women murmured and some wished to flee from Ummaos, and it seemed that the revels of the day and evening were shadowed by ill wings that left their umbrage in the yellow wine and bedimmed the aureate lamps. And again, toward midnight, the slumber of Zotulla was broken by the hooves, which came galloping and pacing on the palace-roof and through all the corridors and the halls. Thereafter, till dawn, the hooves filled the palace with their iron clatterings, and they rung hollowly on the topmost domes, as if the coursers of gods had trodden there, passing from heaven to heaven in tumultuous cavalcade.

Zotulla and Obexah, lying together while the terrible hooves went to and fro in the hall outside their chamber, had no heart or thought for sin, nor could they find any comfort in their nearness. In the gray hour before dawn they heard a great thundering high on the barred brazen door of the room, as if some mighty stallion, rearing, had drummed there with his forefeet. And soon after this, the hooves went away, leaving a silence like an interlude in some gathering storm of doom. Later, the marks of the hooves were found everywhere in the halls, marring the bright mosaics. Black holes were burnt in the golden-threaded rugs and the rugs of silver and scarlet; and the high white domes were pitted pox-wise with the marks; and far up on the brazen door of Zotulla's chamber the prints of a horse's forefeet were incised deeply.

Now, in Ummaos, and throughout Xylac, the tale of this haunting became known, and the thing was deemed an ominous prodigy, though people differed in their interpretations. Some held that the sending came from Namirrha, and was meant as a token of his supremacy above all kings and emperors; and some thought that it came from a new wizard who had risen in Tinarath, far to the east, and who wished to supplant Namirrha. And the priests of the gods of Xylac held that their various deities had dispatched the haunting, as a sign that more sacrifices were required in the temples.

Then, in his hall of audience, whose floor of sard and jasper had been grievously pocked by the unseen hooves, Zotulla called together many priests and magicians and soothsayers, and asked them to declare the cause of the sending and devise a mode of exorcism. But, seeing that there was no agreement among them, Zotulla provided the several priestly sects with the wherewithal of sacrifice to their sundry gods, and sent them away; and the wizards and prophets, under threat of decapitation if they refused, were enjoined to visit Namirrha in his mansion of sorcery and learn his will, if haply the sending were his and not the work of another.

Loth were the wizards and the soothsayers, fearing Namirrha, and caring not to intrude upon the frightful mysteries of his obscure mansion. But the swordsmen of the emperor drove them forth, lifting great crescent blades against them when they tarried; so one by one, in a straggling order, the delegation went towards Namirrha's portals and vanished into the devil-built house.

Pale, muttering and distraught, like men who have looked upon hell and have seen their doom, they returned before sunset to the emperor. And they said that Namirrha had received them courteously and had sent them back with this message:

"Be it known to Zotulla that the haunting is a sign of that which he has long forgotten; and the reason of the haunting will be revealed to him at the hour prepared and set apart by destiny. And the hour draws near: for Namirrha bids the emperor and all his court to a great feast on the afternoon of the morrow."

Having delivered this message, to the wonder and consternation of Zotulla, the delegation begged his leave to depart. And though the emperor questioned them minutely, they seemed unwilling to relate the circumstances of the visit to Namirrha; nor would they describe the sorcerer's fabled house, except in a vague manner, each contradicting the other as to what he had seen. So, after a little, Zotulla bade them go, and when they had gone he sat musing for a long while on the invitation of Namirrha, which was a thing he cared not to accept but feared to decline. That evening he drank even more liberally than was his wont; and he slept a Lethean slumber, nor was there any noise of trampling hooves about the palace to awaken him. And silently, during the night, the prophets and magicians passed like furtive shadows from Ummaos; and no man saw them depart; and at morning they were gone from Xylac into other lands, never to return....

Now, on that same evening, in the great hall of his house, Namirrha sat alone, having dismissed the familiars who attended him ordinarily. Before him, on an altar of jet, was the dark, gigantic statue of Thasaidon which a devil-begotten sculptor had wrought in ancient days for an evil king of Tasuun, called Pharnoc. The archdemon was depicted in the guise of a full-armored warrior, lifting a spiky mace as if in heroic battle. Long had the statue lain in the desert-sunken palace of Pharnoc, whose very site was disputed by the nomads; and Namirrha, by his divination, had found it and had reared up the infernal image to abide with him always thereafter. And often, through the mouth of the statue, Thasaidon would utter oracles to Namirrha, or would answer interrogations.

Before the black-armored image there hung seven silver lamps, wrought in the form of horses' skulls, with flames issuing changeably in blue and purple and crimson from their eye-sockets. Wild and lurid was their light, and the face of the demon, peering from under his crested helmet, was filled with malign, equivocal shadows that shifted and changed eternally. And sitting in his serpent-carven chair, Namirrha regarded the statue grimly, with a deep-furrowed frown between his eyes: for he had asked a certain thing of Thasaidon, and the fiend, replying through the statue, had refused him. And rebellion was in the heart of Namirrha, grown mad with pride, and deeming himself the lord of all sorcerers and a ruler by his own right among the princes of devildom. So, after long pondering, he repeated his request in a bold and haughty voice, like one who addresses an equal rather than the all-formidable suzerain to whom he had sworn a fatal fealty.

"I have helped you heretofore in all things," said the image, with stony and sonorous accents that were echoed metallically in the seven silver lamps. "Yea, the undying worms of fire and darkness have come forth like an army at your summons, and the wings of nether genii have risen to occlude the sun when you called them. But, verily, I will not aid you in this vengeance you have planned: for the emperor Zotulla has done me no wrong and has served me well though unwittingly; and the people of Xylac, by reason of their turpitudes, are not the least of my terrestial worshippers. Therefore, Namirrha, it were well for you to live in peace with Zotulla, and well to forget this olden wrong that was done to the beggar-boy Narthos. For the ways of destiny are strange, and the workings of its laws sometimes hidden; and truly, if the hooves of Zotulla's palfrey had not spurned you and trodden you under, your life had been otherwise, and the name and renown of Namirrha had still slept in oblivion as a dream undreamed. Yea, you would tarry still as a beggar in Ummaos, content with a beggar's guerdon, and would never have fared forth to become the pupil of the wise and learned Ouphaloc; and I, Thasaidon, would have lost the lordliest of all necromancers who have accepted my service and my bond. Think well, Namirrha, and ponder these matters: for both of us, it would seem, are indebted to Zotulla in all gratitude for the trampling he gave you."

"Yea, there is a debt," Namirrha growled implacably. "And truly I will pay the debt tomorrow, even as I have planned.... There are Those who will aid me, Those who will answer my summoning in your despite."

"It is an ill thing to affront me," said the image, after an interval. "And also, it is not wise to call upon Those that you designate. However, I perceive clearly that such is your intent. You are proud and stubborn and revengeful. Do then, as you will, but blame me not for the outcome."

So, after this, there was silence in the hall where Namirrha sat before the eidolon; and the flames burned darkly, with changeable colors, in the skull-shapen lamps; and the shadows fled and returned, unresting, on the face of the statue and the face of Namirrha. Then, toward midnight, the necromancer arose and went upward by many spiral stairs to a high dome of his house in which there was a single small round window that looked forth on the constellations. The window was set in the top of the dome; but Namirrha had contrived, by means of his magic, that one entering by the last spiral of the stairs would suddenly seem to descend rather than climb, and, reaching the last step, would peer downward through the window while stars passed under him in a giddying gulf. There, kneeling, Namirrha touched a secret spring in the marble, and the circular pane slid back without sound. Then, lying prone on the interior of the dome, with his face over the abyss, and his long beard trailing stiffly into space, he whispered a pre-human rune, and held speech with certain entities who belonged neither to Hell nor the mundane elements, and were more fearsome to invoke than the infernal genii or the devils of earth, air, water, and flame. With them he made his contract, defying Thasaidon's will, while the air curdled about him with their voices, and rime gathered palely on his sable beard from the cold that was wrought by their breathing as they leaned earthward.

Laggard and loth was the awakening of Zotulla from his wine; and quickly, ere he opened his eyes, the daylight was poisoned for him by the thought of that invitation which he feared to accept or decline. But he spoke to Obexah, saying:

"Who, after all, is this wizardly dog, that I should obey his summons like a beggar called in from the street by some haughty lord?"

Obexah, a golden-skinned and oblique-eyed girl from Uccastrog, Isle of the Torturers, eyed the emperor subtly, and said:

"O Zotulla, it is yours to accept or refuse, as you deem fitting. And truly, it is a small matter for the lord of Ummaos and all Xylac, whether to go or to stay, since naught can impugn his sovereignty. Therefore, were it not as well to go?" For Obexah, though fearful of the wizard, was curious regarding that devil-builded house of which so little was known; and likewise, in the manner of women, she wished to behold the famed Namirrha, whose mien and appearance were still but a far-brought legend in Ummaos.

"There is something in what you say," admitted Zotulla. "But an emperor, in his conduct, must always consider the public good; and there are matters of state involved, which a woman can scarcely be expected to understand."

So, later in the forenoon, after an ample and well-irrigated breakfast, he called his chamberlains and courtiers about him and took counsel with them. And some advised him to ignore the invitation of Namirrha; and others held that the invitation be accepted, lest a graver evil than the trampling of ghostly hooves be sent upon the palace and the city.

Then Zotulla called the many priesthoods before him in a body, and sought to resummon the wizards and soothsayers who had fled privily in the night. Among all the latter, there was none who answered the crying of his name through Ummaos; and this aroused a certain wonder. But the priests came in a greater number than before, and thronged the hall of audience so that the paunches of the foremost were straightened against the imperial dais and the buttocks of the hindmost were flattened on the rear walls and pillars. And Zotulla debated with them the matter of acceptance or refusal. And the priests argued, as before, that Namirrha was nowherewise concerned with the sending ; and his invitation, they said, portended no harm nor bale to the emperor; and it was plain, from the terms of the message, that an oracle would be imparted to Zotulla by the wizard; and this oracle, if Namirrha were a true archimage, would confirm their own holy wisdom and reëstablish the divine source of the sending; and the gods of Xylac would again be glorified.

Then, having heard the pronouncement of the priests, the emperor instructed his treasurers to load them down with new offerings; and calling unctuously upon Zotulla and all his household the vicarious blessings of the several gods, the priests departed. And the day wore on, and the sun passed its meridian, falling slowly beyond Ummaos through the spaces of the afternoon that were floored with sea-ending deserts. And still Zotulla was irresolute; and he called his wine-bearers, bidding them pour for him the strongest and most magistral of their vintages; but in the wine he found neither certitude nor decision.

Sitting still on his throne in the hall of audience, he heard, toward middle afternoon, a mighty and clamorous outcry that arose at the palace portals. There were deep wailings of men and the shrillings of eunuchs and women, as if terror passed from tongue to tongue, invading the halls and apartments. And the fearful clamor spread throughout all the palace, and Zotulla, rousing from the lethargy of wine, was about to send his attendants to inquire the cause.

Then, into the hall, there filed an array of tall mummies, clad in royal cerements of purple and scarlet, and wearing gold crowns on their withered craniums. And after them, like servitors, came gigantic skeletons who wore loin-cloths of nacarat orange and about whose upper skulls, from brow to crown, live serpents of banded saffron and ebon had wrapped themselves for head-dresses. And the mummies bowed before Zotulla, saying with thin, sere voices:

"We, who were kings of the wide realm of Tasuun aforetime,

have been sent as a guard of honor for the emperor Zotulla, to attend him as is befitting when he goes forth to the feast prepared by Namirrha."

Then with dry clickings of their teeth, and whistlings as of air through screens of fretted ivory, the skeletons spoke:

"We, who were giant warriors of a race forgotten, have also been sent by Namirrha, so that the emperor's household, following him to the feast, should be guarded from all peril and should fare forth in such pageantry as is meet and proper."

Witnessing these prodigies, the wine-bearers and other attendants cowered about the imperial dais or hid behind the pillars, while Zotulla, with pupils swimming starkly in a bloodshot white, with face bloated and ghastly pale, sat frozen on his throne and could utter no word in reply to the ministers of Namirrha.

Then, coming forward, the mummies said in dusty accents: "All is made ready, and the feast awaits the arrival of Zotulla." And the cerements of the mummies stirred and fell open at the bosom, and small rodent monsters, brown as bitumen, eyed as with accursed rubies, reared forth from the eaten hearts of the mummies like rats from their holes and chittered shrilly in human speech, repeating the words. The skeletons in turn took up the solemn sentence; and the black and saffron serpents hissed it from their skulls; and the words were repeated lastly in baleful rumblings by certain furry creatures of dubious form, hitherto unseen by Zotulla, who sat behind the ribs of the skeletons as if in cages of white wicker.

Like a dreamer who obeys the doom of dreams, the emperor rose from his throne and went forward, and the mummies surrounded him like an escort. And each of the skeletons drew from the reddish-yellow folds of his loin-cloth a curiously pierced archaic flute of silver; and all began a sweet and evil and deathly fluting as the emperor went out through the halls of the palace. A fatal spell was in the music: for the chamberlains, the women, the guards, the eunuchs, and all members of Zotulla's household even to the cooks and scullions, were drawn like a procession of night-walkers from the rooms and alcoves in which they had vainly hidden themselves; and marshaled by the flutists, they followed after Zotulla. A strange thing it was to behold this mighty company of people, going forth in the slanted sunlight toward Namirrha's house, with a cortège of dead kings about them, and the blown breath of skeletons thrilling eldritchly in the silver flutes. And little was Zotulla comforted when he found the girl Obexah at his side, moving, as he, in a thralldom of involitent horror, with the rest of his women close behind.

Coming to the open portals of Namirrha's house, the emperor saw that they were guarded by great crimson-wattled things, half dragon, half man, who bowed before him, sweeping their wattles like bloody besoms on the flags of dark onyx. And the emperor passed with Obexah between the louting monsters, with the mummies, the skeletons and his own people behind him in strange pageant, and entered a vast and multicolumned hall, where the daylight, following timidly, was drowned by the baleful arrogant blaze of a thousand lamps.

Even amid his horror, Zotulla marvelled at the vastness of the chamber, which he could hardly reconcile with the mansion's outer length and height and breadth, though these indeed were of most palatial amplitude. For it seemed that he gazed down great avenues of topless pillars, and vistas of tables laden with piled-up viands and thronged urns of wine, that stretched away before him into luminous distance and gloom as of starless night.

In the wide intervals between the tables, the familiars of Namirrha and his other servants went to and fro incessantly, as if a fantasmagoria of ill dreams were embodied before the emperor. Kingly cadavers in robes of time-rotted brocade, with worms seething in their eye-pits, poured a blood-like wine into cups of the opalescent horn of unicorns. Lamias, trident-tailed, and four-breasted chimeras, came in with fuming platters lifted high by their brazen claws. Dog-headed devils, tongued with lolling flames, ran forward to offer themselves as ushers for the company. And before Zotulla and Obexah, there appeared a curious being with the full-fleshed lower limbs and hips of a great black woman and the clean-picked bones of some titanic ape from thereupward.

Verily, it seemed to Zotulla that they had gone a long way into some malignly litten cavern of Hell, when they came to that perspective of tables and columns down which the monster had led them. Here, at the room's end, apart from the rest, was a table at which Namirrha sat alone, with the flames of the seven horse-skull lamps burning restlessly behind him, and the mailed black image of Thasaidon towering from the altar of jet at his right hand. And a little aside from the altar, a diamond mirror was upborne by the claws of iron basilisks.

Namirrha rose to greet them, observing a solemn and funereal courtesy. His eyes were bleak and cold as distant stars in the hollows wrought by strange fearful vigils. His lips were like a pale-red seal on a shut parchment of doom. His beard flowed stiffly in black-anointed banded locks across the bosom of his vermilion robe, like a mass of straight black serpents. Zotulla felt the blood pause and thicken about his heart, as if congealing into ice. And Obexah, peering beneath lowered lids, was abashed and frightened by the visible horror that invested this man and hung upon him even as royalty upon a king. But amid her fear, she found room to wonder what manner of man he was in his intercourse with women.

"I bid you welcome, O Zotulla, to such hospitality as is mine to offer," said Namirrha, with the iron ringing of some hidden funereal bell deep down in his hollow voice. "Prithee, be seated at my table."

Zotulla saw that a chair of ebony had been placed for him opposite Namirrha; and another chair, less stately and imperial, had been placed at the left hand for Obexah. And the twain seated themselves; and Zotulla saw that his people were sitting likewise at other tables throughout the huge hall, with the frightful servants of Namirrha waiting upon them busily, like devils attending the damned.

Then Zotulla perceived that a dark and corpse-like hand was pouring wine for him in a crystal cup; and upon the hand was the signet-ring of the emperors of Xylac, set with a monstrous fire-opal in the mouth of a golden bat: even such a ring as Zotulla wore perpetually on his index-finger. And, turning, he beheld at his right hand a figure that bore the likeness of his father, Pithaim, after the poison of the adder, spreading through his limbs, had left behind it the purple bloating of death. And Zotulla, who had caused the adder to be placed in the bed of Pithaim, cowered in his seat and trembled with a guilty fear. And the thing that wore the similitude of Pithaim, whether corpse or an image wrought by Namirrha's enchantment, came and went at Zotulla's elbow, waiting upon him with stark, black, swollen fingers that never fumbled. Horribly he was aware of its bulging, unregarding eyes, and its livid purple mouth that was locked in a rigor of mortal silence, and the spotted adder that peered at intervals with chill orbs from its heavy-folded sleeve as it leaned beside him to replenish his cup or to serve him with meat. And dimly, through the icy mist of his terror, the emperor beheld the shadowy-armored shape, like a moving replica of the still, grim statue of Thasaidon, which Namirrha had reared up in his blasphemy to perform the same office for himself. And vaguely, without comprehension, he saw the dreadful ministrant that hovered beside Obexah: a flayed and eyeless corpse in the image of her first lover, a boy from Cyntrom who had been cast ashore in shipwreck on the Isle of the Torturers. There Obexah had found him, lying behind the ebbing wave, and reviving the boy, she had hidden him awhile in a secret cave for her own pleasure, and had brought him food and drink. Later, wearying, she had betrayed him to the Torturers, and had taken a new delight in the various pangs and ordeals inflicted upon him before death by that cruel, pernicious people.

"Drink," said Namirrha, quaffing a strange wine that was red and dark as if with disastrous sunsets of lost years. And Zotulla and Obexah drank the wine, feeling no warmth in their veins thereafter, but a chill as of hemlock mounting slowly toward the heart.

"Verily, 'tis a good wine," said Namirrha, "and a proper one in which to toast the furthering of our acquaintance: for it was buried long ago with the royal dead, in amphorae of somber jasper shapen like funeral urns; and my ghouls found it, whenas they came to dig in Tasuun."

Now it seemed that the tongue of Zotulla froze in his mouth, as a mandrake freezes in the rime-bound soil of winter; and he found no reply to Namirrha's courtesy.

"Prithee, make trial of this meat," quoth Namirrha, "for it is very choice, being the flesh of that boar which the Torturers of Uccastrog are wont to pasture on the well-minced leavings of their wheels and racks; and, moreover, my cooks have spiced it with the powerful balsams of the tomb, and have farced it with the hearts of adders and the tongues of black cobras."

Naught could the emperor say; and even Obexah was silent, being sorely troubled in her turpitude by the presence of that flayed and piteous thing which had the likeness of her lover from Cyntrom. And the dread of the necromancer grew prodigiously; for his knowledge of this old, forgotten crime, and the raising of the fantasm, appeared to her a more baleful magic than all else.

"Now, I fear," said Namirrha, "that you find the meat devoid of savor, and the wine without fire. So, to enliven our feasting, I shall call forth my singers and my musicians."

He spoke a word unknown to Zotulla or Obexah, which sounded throughout the mighty hall as if a thousand voices in turn had taken it up and prolonged it. Anon there appeared the singers, who were she-ghouls with shaven bodies and hairy shanks, and long yellow tushes full of shredded carrion curving across their chaps from mouths that fawned hyena-wise on the company. Behind them entered the musicians, some of whom were male devils pacing erect on the hind-quarters of sable stallions and plucking with the fingers of white apes at lyres of the bone and sinew of cannibals from Naat; and others were pied satyrs puffing their goatish cheeks at hautboys formed from the bosom-skin of Negro queens and the horn of rhinoceri.

They bowed before Namirrha with grotesque ceremony. Then, without delay, the she-ghouls began a most dolorous and execrable howling, as of jackals that have sniffed their carrion; and the satyrs and devils played a lament that was like the moaning of desert-born winds through forsaken palace harems. And Zotulla shivered, for the singing filled his marrow with ice, and the music left in his heart a desolation as of empires fallen and trod under by the iron-shod hooves of time. Ever, amid that evil music, he seemed to hear the sifting of sand across withered gardens, and the windy rustling of rotted silks upon couches of bygone luxury, and the hissing of coiled serpents from the low fusts of shattered columns. And the glory that had been Ummaos seemed to pass away like the blown pillars of the simoom.

"Now that was a brave tune," said Namirrha when the music ceased and the she-ghouls no longer howled. "But verily I fear that you find my entertainment somewhat dull. Therefore, my dancers shall dance for you."

He turned toward the great hall, and described in the air an enigmatic sign with the fingers of his right hand. In answer to the sign, a hueless mist came down from the high roof and hid the room like a fallen curtain for a brief interim. There was a babel of sounds, confused and muffled, beyond the curtain, and a crying of voices faint as if with distance.

Then, dreadfully, the vapor rolled away, and Zotulla saw that the leaden tables had gone. In the wide interspaces of the columns, his palace-inmates, the chamberlains, the eunuchs, the courtiers and odalisques and all the others, lay trussed with thongs on the floor, like so many fowls of glorious plumage. Above them, in time to a music made by the lyrists and flutists of the necromancer, a troupe of skeletons pirouetted with light clickings of their toe-bones; and a rout of mummies bowed stiffly; and others of Namirrha's creatures moved with mysterious caperings. To and fro they leapt on the bodies of the emperor's people, in the paces of an evil saraband. At every step they grew taller and heavier, till the saltant mummies were as the mummies of Anakim, and the skeletons were boned as colossi; and louder the music rose, drowning the faint cries of Zotulla's people. And huger still became the dancers, towering far into vaulted shadow among the vast columns, with thudding feet that wrought thunder in the room; and those whereon they danced were as grapes trampled for a vintage in autumn; and the floor ran deep with a sanguine must.

As a man drowning in a noisome, night-bound fen, the emperor heard the voice of Namirrha:

"It would seem that my dancers please you not. So now I shall present you a most royal spectacle. Arise and follow me, for the spectacle is one that requires an empire for its stage."

Zotulla and Obexah rose from their chairs in the fashion of night-walkers. Giving no backward glance at their ministering phantoms, or the hall where the dancers bounded, they followed Namirrha to an alcove beyond the altar of Thasaidon. Thence, by the upward-coiling stairways, they came at length to a broad high balcony that faced Zotulla's palace and looked forth above the city roofs toward the bourn of sunset.

It seemed that several hours had gone by in that hellish feasting and entertainment; for the day was near to its close, and the sun, which had fallen from sight behind the imperial palace, was barring the vast heavens with bloody rays.

"Behold," said Namirrha, adding a strange vocable to which the stone of the edifice resounded like a beaten gong.

The balcony pitched a little, and Zotulla, looking over the balustrade, beheld the roofs of Ummaos lessen and sink beneath him. It seemed that the balcony flew skyward to a prodigious height, and he peered down across the domes of his own palace, upon the houses, the tilled fields and the desert beyond, and the huge sun brought low on the desert's verge. And Zotulla grew giddy; and the chill airs of the upper heavens blew upon him. But Namirrha spoke another word, and the balcony ceased to ascend.

"Look well," said the necromancer, "on the empire that was yours, but shall be yours no longer." Then, with arms outstretched toward the sunset, he called aloud the twelve names that were perdition to utter, and after them the tremendous invocation: Gna padambis devompra thungis furidor avoragomon.

Instantly, it seemed that great ebon clouds of thunder beetled against the sun. Lining the horizon, the clouds took the form of colossal monsters with heads and members somewhat resembling those of stallions. Rearing terribly, they trod down the sun like an extinguished ember; and racing as if in some hippodrome of Titans, they rose higher and vaster, coming towards Ummaos. Deep, calamitous rumblings preceded them, and the earth shook visibly, till Zotulla saw that these were not immaterial clouds, but actual living forms that had come forth to tread the world in macrocosmic vastness. Throwing their shadows for many leagues before them, the coursers charged as if devil-ridden into Xylac, and their feet descended like falling mountain crags upon far oases and towns of the outer wastes.Like a many-turreted storm they came, and it seemed that the world shrank gulfward, tilting beneath the weight.

Still as a man enchanted into marble, Zotulla stood and beheld the ruining that was wrought on his empire. And closer drew the gigantic stallions, racing with inconceivable speed, and louder was the thundering of their footfalls, that now began to blot the green fields and fruited orchards lying for many miles to the west of Ummaos. And the shadow of the stallions climbed like an evil gloom of eclipse, till it covered Ummaos; and looking up, the emperor saw their eyes halfway between earth and zenith, like baleful suns that glare down from soaring cumuli.

Then, in the thickening gloom, above that insupportable thunder, he heard the voice of Namirrha, crying in mad triumph:

"Know, Zotulla, that I have called up the coursers of Thamogorgos, lord of the abyss. And the coursers will tread your empire down, even as your palfrey trod and trampled in former time a beggar-boy named Narthos. And learn also that I, Namirrha, was that boy." And the eyes of Namirrha, filled with a vainglory of madness and bale, burned like malign, disastrous stars at the hour of their culmination.

To Zotulla, wholly mazed with the horror and tumult, the necromancer's words were no more than shrill, shrieked overtones of the tempest of doom; and he understood them not. Tremendously, with a rending of staunch-built roofs, and an instant cleavage and crumbling down of mighty masonries, the hooves descended upon Ummaos. Fair temple-domes were pashed like shells of the haliotis, and haughty mansions were broken and stamped into the ground even as gourds; and house by house the city was trampled flat with a crashing as of worlds beaten into chaos. Far below, in the darkened streets, men and camels fled like scurrying emmets but could not escape. And implacably the hooves rose and fell, till ruin was upon half the city, and night was over all. The palace of Zotulla was trodden under, and now the forelegs of the coursers loomed level with Namirrha's balcony, and their heads towered awfully above. It seemed that they would rear and trample down the necromancer's house; but at that moment they parted to left and right, and a dolorous glimmering came from the low sunset; and the coursers went on, treading under them that portion of Ummaos which lay to the eastward. And Zotulla and Obexah and Namirrha looked down on the city's fragments as on a shard-strewn midden, and heard the cataclysmic clamor of the hooves departing toward eastern Xylac.

"Now that was a goodly spectacle," quoth Namirrha. Then, turning to the emperor, he added malignly: "Think not that I have done with thee, however, or that doom is yet consummate."

It seemed that the balcony had fallen to its former elevation, which was still a lofty vantage above the sharded ruins. And Namirrha plucked the emperor by the arm and led him from the balcony to an inner chamber, while Obexah followed mutely. The emperor's heart was crushed within him by the trampling of such calamities, and despair weighed upon him like a foul incubus on the shoulders of a man lost in some land of accursed night. And he knew not that he had been parted from Obexah on the threshold of the chamber, and that certain of Namirrha's creatures, appearing like shadows, had compelled the girl to go downward with them by the stairs, and had stifled her outcries with their rotten cerements as they went.

The chamber was one that Namirrha used for his most unhallowed rites and alchemies. The rays of the lamps that illumed it were saffron-red like the spilt ichor of devils, and they flowed on aludels and crucibles and black athanors and alembics whereof the purpose was hardly to be named by mortal man. The sorcerer heated in one of the alembics a dark liquid full of star-cold lights, while Zotulla looked on unheeding. And when the liquid bubbled and sent forth a spiral vapor, Namirrha distilled it into goblets of gold-rimmed iron, and gave one of the goblets to Zotulla and retained the other himself. And he said to Zotulla with a stern imperative voice: "I bid thee quaff this liquor."

Zotulla, fearing that the draft was poison, hesitated. And the necromancer regarded him with a lethal gaze, and cried loudly: "Fearest thou to do as I?" and therewith he set the goblet to his lips.

So the emperor drank the draft, constrained as if by the bidding of some angel of death, and a darkness fell upon his senses. But, ere the darkness grew complete, he saw that Namirrha had drained his own goblet.

Then, with unspeakable agonies, it seemed that the emperor died; and his soul float free; and again he saw the chamber, though with bodiless eyes. And discarnate he stood in the saffron-crimson light, with his body lying as if dead on the floor beside him, and near it the prone body of Namirrha and the two fallen goblets.

Standing thus, he beheld a strange thing: for anon his own body stirred and arose, while that of the necromancer remained still as death. And Zotulla looked at his own lineaments and his figure in its short cloak of azure samite sewn with black pearls and balas-rubies; and the body lived before him, though with eyes that held a darker fire and a deeper evil than was their wont. Then, without corporeal ears, Zotulla heard the figure speak, and the voice was the strong, arrogant voice of Namirrha, saying:

"Follow me, O houseless phantom, and do in all things as I

enjoin thee."

Like an unseen shadow, Zotulla followed the wizard, and the twain went downward by the stairs to the great banquet hall. They came to the altar of Thasaidon and the mailed image, with the seven horse-skull lamps burning before it as formerly. Upon the altar, Zotulla's beloved leman Obexah, who alone of all women had power to stir his sated heart, was lying bound with thongs at Thasaidon's feet. But the hall beyond was deserted, and nothing remained of that Saturnalia of doom except the fruit of the treading, which had flowed together in dark pools among the columns.

Namirrha, using the emperor's body in all ways for his own, paused before the dark eidolon; and he said to the spirit of Zotulla: "Be imprisoned in this image, without power to free thyself or to stir in any wise."

Being wholly obedient to the will of the necromancer, the soul of Zotulla was embodied in the statue, and he felt its cold, gigantic armor about him like a straight sarcophagus, and he peered forth immovably from the bleak eyes that were overhung by its carven helmet.

Gazing thus, he beheld the change that had come on his own body through the sorcerous possession of Namirrha: for below the short azure cloak, the legs had turned suddenly to the hind legs of a black stallion, with hooves that glowed redly as if heated by infernal fires. And even as Zotulla watched this prodigy, the hooves glowed white and incandescent, and fumes mounted from the floor beneath them.

Then, on the black altar, the hybrid abomination came pacing haughtily toward Obexah, and smoking footprints appeared behind it as it came. Pausing beside the girl, who lay supine and helpless regarding it with eyes that were pools of frozen horror, it raised one glowing hoof and set the hoof on her naked bosom between the small breast-cups of golden filigree begemmed with rubies. And the girl screamed beneath that atrocious treading as the soul of one newly damned might scream in hell; and the hoof glared with intolerable brilliance, as if freshly plucked from a furnace wherein the weapons of demons were forged.

At that moment, in the cowed and crushed and sodden shade of the emperor Zotulla, close-locked within the adamantine image, there awoke the manhood that had slumbered unaroused before the ruining of his empire and the trampling of his retinue. Immediately a great abhorrence and a high wrath were alive in his soul, and mightily he longed for his own right arm to serve him, and a sword in his right hand.

Then it seemed that a voice spoke within him, chill and bleak and awful, and as if uttered inwardly by the statue itself. And the voice said: "I am Thasaidon, lord of the seven hells beneath the earth, and the hells of man's heart above the earth, which are seven times seven. For the moment, O Zotulla, my power is become thine for the sake of a mutual vengeance. Be one in all ways with the statue that has my likeness, even as the soul is one with the flesh. Behold! there is a mace of adamant in thy right hand. Lift up the mace, and smite."

Zotulla was aware of a great power within him, and giant thews about him that thrilled with the power and responded agilely to his will. He felt in his mailed right hand the haft of the huge spiky-headed mace; and though the mace was beyond the lifting of any man in mortal flesh, it seemed no more than a goodly weight to Zotulla. Then, rearing he mace like a warrior in battle, he struck down with one crashing blow the impious thing that wore his own rightful flesh united with the legs and hooves of a demon courser. And the thing crumpled swiftly down and lay with the brain spreading pulpily from its shattered skull on the shining jet. And the legs twitched a little and then grew still; and the hooves glowed from a fiery, blinding white to the redness of red-hot iron, cooling slowly.

For a space there was no sound, other than the shrill screaming of the girl Obexah, mad with pain and the terror of those prodigies which she had beheld. Then in the soul of Zotulla, grown sick with that screaming, the chill, awful voice of Thasaidon spoke again:

"Go free, for there is nothing more for thee to do." So the spirit of Zotulla passed from the image of Thasaidon and found in the wide air the freedom of nothingness and oblivion.

But the end was not yet for Namirrha, whose mad, arrogant soul had been loosened from Zotulla's body by the blow, and had returned darkly, not in the manner planned by the magician, to its own body lying in the room of accursed rites and forbidden trans-migrations. There Namirrha woke anon, with a dire confusion in his mind, and a partial forgetfulness: for the curse of Thasaidon was upon him now because of his blasphemies.

Nothing was clear in his thought except a malign, exorbitant longing for revenge; but the reason thereof, and the object, were as doubtful shadows. And still prompted by that obscure animus, he arose; and girding to his side an enchanted sword with runic sapphires and opals in the hilt, he descended the stairs and came again to the altar of Thasaidon, where the mailed statue stood as impassive as before, with the poised mace in its immovable right hand,

and below it, on the altar, the double sacrifice.

A veil of weird darkness was upon the senses of Namirrha, and he saw not the stallion-legged horror that lay dead with slowly blackening hooves; and he heard not the moaning of the girl Obexah, who still lived beside it. But his eyes were drawn by the diamond mirror that was upheld in the claws of black iron basilisks beyond the altar; and going to the mirror, he saw therein a face that he knew no longer for his own. And because his eyes were shadowed and his brain filled with the shifting webs of delusion, he took the face for that of the emperor Zotulla. Insatiable as Hell's own flame, his old hatred rose within him; and he drew the enchanted sword and began to hew therewith at the reflection. Sometimes, because of the curse laid upon him, and the impious transmigration which he had performed, he thought himself Zotulla warring with the necromancer; and again, in the shiftings of his madness, he was Namirrha smiting at the emperor; and then, without name, he fought a nameless foe. And soon the sorcerous blade, though tempered with formidable spells, was broken close to the hilt, and Namirrha beheld the image still unharmed. Then, howling aloud the half-forgotten runes of a most tremendous curse, made invalid through his own forgettings, he hammered still with the heavy sword-hilt on the mirror, till the runic sapphires and opals cracked in the hilt and fell away at his feet in little fragments.

Obexah, dying on the altar, saw Namirrha battling with his image, and the spectacle moved her to mad laughter like the pealing of bells of ruined crystal. And above her laughter, and above the cursings of Namirrha, there came anon like the rumbling of a swift-driven storm the thunder made by the macrocosmic stallions of Thamogorgos, returning gulfward through Xylac over Ummaos, to trample down the one house that they had spared aforetime.

THE CHARNEL GOD

|| Mordiggian is the god of Zul-Bha-Sair," said the innkeeper with unctuous solemnity. "He has been the god from years that are lost to man's memory in shadow deeper than the subterranes of his black temple. There is no other god in Zul-Bha-Sair. And all who die within the walls of the city are sacred to Mordiggian. Even the kings and the optimates, at death, are delivered into the hands of his muffled priests. It is the law and the custom. A little while, and the priests will come for your bride."

"But Elaith is not dead," protested the youth Phariom for the third or fourth time, in piteous desperation. "Her malady is one that assumes the lying likeness of death. Twice before has she lain insensible, with a pallor upon her cheeks and a stillness in her very blood, that could hardly be distinguished from those of the tomb; and twice she has awakened after an interim of days."

The innkeeper peered with an air of ponderous unbelief at the girl who lay white and motionless as a mown lily on the bed in the poorly furnished attic chamber.

"In that case you should not have brought her into Zul-Bha-Sair," he averred in a tone of owlish irony. "The physician has pronounced her dead; and her death has been reported to the priests. She must go to the temple of Mordiggian."

"But we are outlanders, guests of a night. We have come from the land of Xylac, far in the north; and this morning we should have gone on through Tasuun, toward Pharaad, the capital of Yoros, which lies near to the southern sea. Surely your god could have no claim upon Elaith, even if she were truly dead."

"All who die in Zul-Bha-Sair are the property of Mordiggian," insisted the taverner sententiously. "Outlanders are not exempt. The dark maw of his temple yawns eternally, and no man, no child, no woman, throughout the years, has evaded its yawning. All mortal flesh must become, in due time, the provender of the god."

Phariom shuddered at the oily and portentous declaration.

"Dimly have I heard of Mordiggian, as a legend that travellers tell in Xylac," he admitted. "But I had forgotten the name of his city; and Elaith and I came ignorantly into Zul-Bha-Sair... Even had I known, I should have doubted the terrible custom of which you inform me. ...What manner of deity is this, who imitates the hyena and the vulture? Surely he is no god, but a ghoul."

"Take heed lest you utter blasphemy," admonished the innkeeper. "Mordiggian is old and omnipotent as death. He was worshipped in former continents, before the lifting of Zothique from out the sea. Through him, we are saved from corruption and the worm. Even as the people of other places devote their dead to the consuming flame, so we of Zul-Bha-Sair deliver ours to the god. Awful is the fane, a place of terror and obscure shadow untrod by the sun, into which the dead are borne by his priests and are laid on a vast table of stone to await his coming from the nether vault in which he dwells. No living men, other than the priests, have ever beheld him; and the faces of the priests are hidden behind masks of silver, and even their hands are shrouded, that men may not gaze on them that have seen Mordiggian."

"But there is a king in Zul-Bha-Sair, is there not? I shall appeal to him against this heinous and horrible injustice. Surely he will heed me."

"Phenquor is the king; but he could not help you even if he wished. Your appeal will not even be heard. Mordiggian is above all kings, and his law is sacred. Hark! — for already the priests come."

Phariom, sick at heart with the charnel terror and cruelty of the doom that impended for his girlish wife in this unknown city of nightmare, heard an evil, stealthy creaking on the stairs that led to the attic of the inn. The sound drew nearer with inhuman rapidity, and four strange figures came into the room, heavily garbed in funereal purple, and wearing huge masks of silver graven in the likeness of skulls. It was impossible to surmise their actual appearance, for, even as the taverner had hinted, their very hands were concealed by fingerless gloves; and the purple gowns came down in loose folds that trailed about their feet like unwinding cerecloths. There was a horror about them, of which the macabre masks were only a lesser element; a horror that lay partly in their unnatural, crouching attitudes, and the beastlike agility with which they moved, unhampered by their cumbrous habiliments.

Among them, they carried a curious bier, made from interwoven strips of leather, and with monstrous bones that served for frame and handles. The leather was greasy and blackened as if from long years of mortuary use. Without speaking to Phariom or the innkeeper, and with no delay or formality of any sort, they advanced toward the bed on which Elaith was lying.

Undeterred by their more than formidable aspect, and wholly distraught with grief and anger, Phariom drew from his girdle a short knife, the only weapon he possessed. Disregarding the minatory cry of the taverner, he rushed wildly upon the muffled figures. He was quick and muscular, and, moreover, was clad in light, close-fitting raiment, such as would seemingly have given him a brief advantage.

The priests had turned their backs upon him; but, as if they had foreseen his every action, two of them wheeled about with the swiftness of tigers, dropping the handles of bone that they carried. One of them struck the knife from Phariom's hand with a movement that the eye could barely follow in its snaky darting. Then both assailed him, beating him back with terrible flailing blows of their shrouded arms, and hurling him half across the room into an empty corner. Stunned by his fall, he lay senseless for a term of minutes.

Recovering glazedly, with eyes that blurred as he opened them, he beheld the fact of the stout taverner stooping above him like a tallow-colored moon. The thought of Elaith, more sharp than the thrust of a dagger, brought him back to agonizing consciousness. Fearfully he scanned the shadowy room, and, saw that the cemented priests were gone, that the bed was vacant. He heard the orotund and sepulchral croaking of the taverner.

"The priests of Mordiggian are merciful, they make allowance for the frenzy and distraction of the newly bereaved. It is well for you that they are compassionate, and considerate of mortal weakness."

Phariom sprang erect, as if his bruised and aching body were scorched by a sudden fire. Pausing only to retrieve his knife, which still lay in the middle of the room, he started toward the door. He was stopped by the hand of the hosteler, clutching greasily at his shoulder.

"Beware, lest you exceed the bounds of the mercy of Mordiggian. It is an ill thing to follow his priests — and a worse thing to intrude upon the deathly and sacred gloom of his temple."

Phariom scarcely heard the admonition. He wrenched himself hastily away from the odious fingers and turned to go; but again the hand clutched him.

"At least, pay me the money that you owe for food and lodging, ere you depart," demanded the innkeeper. "Also, there is the matter of the physician's fee, which I can settle for you, if you will entrust me with the proper sum. Pay now — for there is no surety that you will return."

Phariom drew out the purse that contained his entire worldly wealth, and filled the greedily cupped palm before him with coins that he did not pause to count. With no parting word or backward glance, he descended the moldy and musty stairs of the worm-eaten hostelry, as if spurred by an incubus, and went out into the gloomy, serpentine streets of Zul-Bha-Sair.

Perhaps the city differed little from others, except in being older and darker; but to Phariom, in his extremity of anguish, the ways that he followed were like subterrene corridors that led only to some profound and monstrous charnel. The sun had risen above the overjutting houses, but it seemed to him that there was no light, other than a lost and doleful glimmering such as might descend into mortuary depths. The people, it may have been, were much like other people, but he saw them under a malefic aspect, as if they were ghouls and demons that went to and fro on the ghastly errands of a necropolis.

Bitterly, in his distraction, he recalled the previous evening, when he had entered Zul-Bha-Sair at twilight with Elaith, the girl riding on the one dromedary that had survived their passage of the northern desert, and he walking beside her, weary but content. With the rosy purple of afterglow upon its walls and cupolas, with the deepening golden eyes of its lit windows, the place had seemed a fair and nameless city of dreams, and they had planned to rest there for a day or two before resuming the long, arduous journey to Pharaad, in Yoros.

This journey had been undertaken only through necessity. Phariom, an impoverished youth of noble blood, had been exiled because of the political and religious tenets of his family, which were not in accord with those of the reigning emperor, Caleppos. Taking his newly wedded wife, Phariom had set out for Yoros, where certain allied branches of the house to which he belonged had already established themselves, and would give him a fraternal welcome.

They had travelled with a large caravan of merchants, going directly southward to Tasuun. Beyond the borders of Xylac, amid the red sands of the Celotian waste, the caravan had been attacked by robbers, who had slain many of its members and dispersed the rest. Phariom and his bride, escaping with their dromedaries, had found themselves lost and alone in the desert, and, failing to regain the road toward Tasuun, had taken inadvertently another track, leading to Zul-Bha-Sair, a walled metropolis on the south-western verge of the waste, which their itinerary had not included.

Entering Zul-Bha-Sair, the couple had repaired for reasons of economy to a tavern in the humbler quarter. There, during the night, Elaith had been overcome by the third seizure of the cataleptic malady to which she was liable. The earlier seizures, occurring before her marriage to Phariom, had been recognized in their true character by the physicians of Xylac, and had been palliated by skillful treatment. It was hoped that the malady would not recur.

The third attack, no doubt, had been induced by the fatigues and hardships of the journey. Phariom had felt sure that Elaith would recover, but a doctor of Zul-Bha-Sair, hastily summoned by the innkeeper, had insisted that she was actually dead; and, in obedience to the strange law of the city, had reported her without delay to the priests of Mordiggian. The frantic protests of the husband had been utterly ignored.

There was, it seemed, a diabolic fatality about the whole train of circumstances through which Elaith, still living, though with that outward aspect of the tomb which her illness involved, had fallen into the grasp of the devotees of the charnel god. Phariom pondered this fatality almost to madness, as he strode with furious, aimless haste along the eternally winding and crowded streets.

To the cheerless information received from the taverner, he added, as he went on, more and more of the tardily remembered legends which he had heard in Xylac. Ill and dubious indeed was the renown of Zul-Bha-Sair, and he marvelled that he should have forgotten it, and cursed himself with black curses for the temporary but fatal forgetfulness. Better would it have been if he and Elaith had perished in the desert, rather than enter the wide gates that stood always open, gaping for their prey, as was the custom of Zul-Bha-Sair.

The city was a mart of trade, where outland travelers came, but did not care to linger, because of the repulsive cult of Mordiggian, the invisible eater of the dead, who was believed to share his provender with the shrouded priests. It was said that the bodies lay for days in the dark temple and were not devoured till corruption had begun. And people whispered of fouler things than necrophagism, of blasphemous rites that were solemnized in the ghoul-ridden vaults, and nameless uses to which the dead were put before Mordiggian claimed them. In all outlying places, the fate of those who died in Zul-Bha-Sair was a dreadful byword and a malediction. But to the people of that city, reared in the faith of the ghoulish god, it was merely the usual and expected mode of mortuary disposal. Tombs, graves, catacombs, funeral pyres, and other such nuisances, were rendered needless by this highly utilitarian deity.

Phariom was surprised to see the people of the city going about the common businesses of life. Porters were passing with bales of household goods upon their shoulders. Merchants were squatting in their shops like other merchants. Buyers and sellers chaffered loudly in the public bazaars. Women laughed and chattered in the door ways. Only by their voluminous robes of red, black and violet, and their strange, uncouth accents, was he able to distinguish the men of Zul-Bha-Sair from those who were outlanders like himself. The murk of nightmare began to lift from his impressioms; and gradually, as he went on, the spectacle of everyday humanity all about him helped to calm a little his wild distraction and desperation. Nothing could dissipate the horror of his loss, and the abominable fate that threatened Elaith. But now, with a cool logic born of the cruel exigence, he began to consider the apparently hopeless problem of rescuing her from the ghoul god's temple.

He composed his features, and constrained his febrile pacing to an idle saunter, so that none might guess the preoccupations that racked him inwardly. Pretending to be interested in the wares of a seller of men's apparel, he drew the dealer into converse regarding Zul-Bha-Sair and its customs, and made such inquiries as a traveler from far lands might make. The dealer was talkative, and Phariom soon learned from him the location of the temple of Mordiggian, which stood at the city's core. He also learned that the temple was open at all hours, and that people were free to come and go within its precincts. There were, however, no rituals of worship, other than certain private rites that were celebrated by the priesthood. Few cared to enter the fane, because of a superstition that any living person who intruded upon its gloom would return to it shortly as the provender of the god.

Mordiggian, it seemed, was a benign deity in the eyes of the inhabitants of Zul-Bha-Sair. Curiously enough, no definite personal attributes were ascribed to him. He was, so to speak, an impersonal force akin to the elements — a consuming and cleansing power, like fire. His hierophants were equally mysterious; they lived at the temple and emerged from it only in the execution of their funeral duties. No one knew the manner of their recruiting, but many believed that they were both male and female, thus renewing their numbers from generation to generation with no ulterior commerce. Others thought that they were not human beings at all, but an order of subterranean earth-entities, who lived for ever, and who fed upon corpses like the god himself. Through this latter belief, of late years, a minor heresy had risen, some holding that Mordiggian was a mere hieratic figment, and the priests were the sole devourers of the dead. The dealer, quoting this heresy, made haste to disavow it with pious reprobation.

Phariom chatted for awhile on other topics, and then continued his progress through the city, going as forthrightly toward the temple as the obliquely running thoroughfares would permit. He had formed no conscious plan, but desired to reconnoiter the vicinage. In that which the garment-dealer had told him, the one reassuring detail was the openness of the fane and its accessibility to all who dared enter. The rarity of visitors, however, would make Phariom conspicuous, and he wished above all to avoid attention. On the other hand, any effort to remove bodies from the temple was seemingly unheard of — a thing audacious beyond the dreams of the people of Zul-Bha-Sair. Through the very boldness of his design, he might avoid suspicion, and succeed in rescuing Elaith.

The streets that he followed began to tend downward, and were narrower, dimmer and more tortuous than any he had yet traversed. He thought for awhile that he had lost his way, and he was about to ask the passersby to redirect him, when four of the priests of Mordiggian, bearing one of the curious litter-like biers of bone and leather, emerged from an ancient alley just before him.

The bier was occupied by the body of a girl, and for one moment of convulsive shock and agitation that left him trembling, Phariom thought that the girl was Elaith. Looking again, he saw his mistake. The gown that the girl wore, though simple, was made of some rare exotic stuff. Her features, though pale as those of Elaith, were crowned with curls like the petals of heavy black poppies. Her beauty, warm and voluptuous even in death, differed from the blond pureness of Elaith as tropic lilies differ from narcissi.

Quietly, and maintaining a discreet interval, Phariom followed the sullenly shrouded figures and their lovely burden. He saw that people made way for the passage of the bier with awed, unquestioning alacrity; and the loud voices of hucksters and chafferers were hushed as the priests went by. Overhearing a murmured conversation between two of the townsfolk, he learned that the dead girl was Arctela, daughter of Quaos, a high noble and magistrate of Zul-Bha-Sair. She had died very quickly and mysteriously, from a cause unknown to the physicians, which had not marred or wasted her beauty in the least. There were those who held that an indetectable poison, rather than disease, had been the agency of death; and others deemed her the victim of malefic sorcery.

The priests went on, and Phariom kept them in sight as well as he could in the blind tangle of streets. The way steepened, without affording any clear prospect of the levels below, and the houses seemed to crowd more closely, as if huddling back from a precipice. Finally the youth emerged behind his macabre guides in a sort of circular hollow at the city's heart, where the temple of Mordiggian loomed alone and separate amid pavements of sad onyx, and funerary cedars whose green had blackened as if with the undeparting charnel shadows bequeathed by dead ages.

The edifice was built of a strange stone, hued as with the

blackish purple of carnal decay: a stone that refused the ardent luster of noon, and the prodigality of dawn or sunset glory. It was low and windowless, having the form of a monstrous mausoleum. Its portals yawned sepulchrally in the gloom of the cedars.

Phariom watched the priests as they vanished within the portals, carrying the girl Arctela like phantoms who bear a phantom burden. The broad area of pavement between the recoiling houses and the temple was now deserted, but he did not venture to cross it in the blare of betraying daylight. Circling the area, he saw that there were several other entrances to the great fane, all open and unguarded. There was no sign of activity about the place; but he shuddered at the thought of that which was hidden within its walls, even as the feasting of worms is hidden in the marble tomb.

Like a vomiting of charnels, the abominations of which he had heard rose up before him in the sunlight; and again he drew close to madness, knowing that Elaith must lie among the dead, in the temple, with the foul umbrage of such things upon her, and that he, consumed with unremitting frenzy, must wait for the favorable shrouding of darkness before he could execute his nebulous, doubtful plan of rescue. In the meanwhile, she might awake, and perish from the mortal horror of her surroundings... or worse even than this might befall, if the whispered tales were true...

Abnon-Tha, sorcerer and necromancer, was felicitating himself on the bargain he had made with the priests of Mordiggian. He felt, perhaps justly, that no one less clever than he could have conceived and executed the various procedures that had made possible this bargain, through which Arctela, daughter of the proud Quaos, would became his unquestioning slave. No other lover, he told himself, could have been resourceful enough to obtain a desired woman in this fashion. Arctela, betrothed to Alos, a young noble of the city, was seemingly beyond the aspiration of a sorcerer. Abnon-Tha, however, was no common hedge-wizard, but an adept of long standing in the most awful and profound arcana of the black arts. He knew the spells that kill more quickly and surely than knife or poison, at a distance; and he knew also the darker spells by which the dead can be reanimated, even after years or ages of decay. He had slain Arctela in a manner that none could detect, with a rare and subtle invultuation that had left no mark; and her body lay now among the dead, in Mordiggian's temple. Tonight, with the tacit connivance of the terrible, shrouded priests, he would bring her back to life.

Abnon-Tha was not native to Zul-Bha-Sair, but had come many years before from the infamous, half-mythic isle of Sotar, lying somewhere to the east of the huge continent of Zothique. Like a sleek young vulture, he had established himself in the very shadow of the charnel fane, and had prospered, taking to himself pupils and assistants.

His dealings with the priests were long and extensive, and the bargain he had just made was far from being the first of its kind. They had allowed him the temporary use of bodies claimed by Mordiggian, stipulating only that these bodies should not be removed from the temple during the course of any of his experiments in necromancy. Since the privilege was slightly irregular from their viewpoint, he had found it necessary to bribe them — not, however, with gold, but with the promise of a liberal purveyance of matters more sinister and corruptible than gold. The arrangement had been satisfactory enough to all concerned: cadavers had poured into the temple with more than their usual abundance ever since the coming of the sorcerer; the god had not lacked for provender; and Abnon-Tha had never lacked for subjects on which to employ his more baleful spells.

On the whole, Abnon-Tha was not ill-pleased with himself. He reflected, moreover, that, aside from his mastery of magic and his sleightful ingenuity, he was about to manifest a well-nigh unexampled courage. He had planned a robbery that would amount to dire sacrilege: the removal of the reanimated body of Arctela from the temple. Such robberies (either of animate or exanimate corpses) and the penalty attached to them, were a matter of legend only; for none had occurred in recent ages. Thrice terrible, according to common belief, was the doom of those who had tried and failed. The necromancer was not blind to the risks of his enterprise; nor, on the other hand, was he deterred or intimidated by them.

His two assistants, Narghai and Vemba-Tsith, apprised of his intention, had made with all due privity the necessary preparations for their flight from Zul-Bha-Sair. The strong passion that the sorcerer had conceived for Arctela was not his only motive, perhaps, in removing from that city. He was desirous of change, for he had grown a little weary of the odd laws that really served to restrict his necromantic practices, while facilitating them in a sense. He planned to travel southward, and establish himself in one of the cities of Tasuun, an empire famous for the number and antiquity of its mummies.

It was now sunset-time. Five dromedaries, bred for racing, waited in the inner courtyard of Abnon-Tha's house, a high and moldering mansion that seemed to lean forward upon the open, circular area belonging to the temple. One of the dromedaries would carry a bale containing the sorcerer's most valuable books, manuscripts, and other impedimenta of magic. Its fellows would bear Abnon-Tha, the two assistants — and Arctela.

Narghai and Vemba-Tsith appeared before their master to tell him that all was made ready. Both were much younger than Abnon-Tha; but, like himself, they were outlanders in Zul-Bha-Sair. They came of the swart and narrow-eyed people of Naat, an isle that was little less infamous than Sotar.

"It is well," said the necromancer, as they stood before him with lowered eyes, after making their announcement. "We have only to await the favorable hour. Midway between sunset and moonrise, when the priests are at their supper in the nether adytum, we will enter the temple and perform that which must be done for the rising of Arctela. They feed well tonight, for I know that many of the dead grow ripe on the great table in the upper sanctuary; and it may be that Mordiggian feeds also. None will come to watch us at our doings."

"But, master," said Narghai, shivering a little beneath his robe of nacarat red, "is it wise, after all, to do this thing? Must you take the girl from the temple? Always, ere this, you have contented yourself with the brief loan that the priests allow, and have rendered back the dead in the required state of exanimation. Truly, is it well to violate the law of the god? Men say that the wrath of Mordiggian, though seldom loosed, is more dreadful than the wrath of all other deities. For this reason, none has dared to defraud him in latter years, or attempt the removal of any of the corpses from his fane. Long ago, it is told, a high noble of the city bore hence the cadaver of a woman he had loved, and fled with it into the desert; but the priests pursued him, running more swiftly than jackals ...and the fate that overtook him is a thing whereof the legends whisper but dimly."

"I fear neither Mordiggian nor his creatures," said Abnon-Tha, with a solemn vainglory in his voice. "My dromedaries can outrun the priests — even granting that the priests are not men at all, but ghouls, as some say. And there is small likelihood that they will follow us: after their feasting tonight, they will sleep like gorged vultures The morrow will find us far on the road to Tasuun, ere they awake."

"The master is right," interpolated Vemba-Tsith, "We have nothing to fear."

"But they say that Mordiggian does not sleep," insisted Narghai, "and that he watches all things eternally from his black vault beneath the temple."

"So I have heard," said Abnon-Tha, with a dry and learned air. "But I consider that such beliefs are mere superstition. There is nothing to confirm them in the real nature of corpse-eating entities. So far, I have never beheld Mordiggian, either sleeping or awake; but in all likelihood he is merely a common ghoul. I know these demons and their habits. They differ from hyenas only through their monstrous shape and size, and their immortality."

"Still, I must deem it an ill thing to cheat Mordiggian," muttered Narghai beneath his breath.

The words were caught by the quick ears of AbnonTha. "Nay, there is no question of cheating. Well have I served Mordiggian and his priesthood, and amply have I larded their black table. Also, I shall keep, in a sense, the bargain I have made concerning Arctela: the providing of a new cadaver in return for my necromantic privilege. Tomorrow, the youth Alos, the betrothed of Arctela, will lie in her place among the dead. Go now, and leave me, for I must devise the inward invultuation that will rot the heart of Alos, like a worm that awakens at the core of fruit."

To Phariom, fevered and distraught, it seemed that the cloudless day went by with the sluggishness of a corpse-clogged river. Unable to calm his agitation, he wandered aimlessly through the thronged bazaars, till the western towers grew dark on a heaven of saffron flame, and the twilight rose like a gray and curdling sea among the houses. Then he returned to the inn where Elaith had been stricken, and claimed the dromedary which he had left in the tavern stables. Riding the animal through dim thoroughfares, lit only by the covert gleam of lamps or tapers from half-closed windows, he found his way once more to the city's center.

The dusk had thickened into darkness when he came to the open area surrounding Mordiggian's temple. The windows of mansions fronting the area were shut and lightless as dead eyes, and the fane itself, a colossal bulk of gloom, was rayless as any mausoleum beneath the gathering stars. No one, it seemed, was abroad, and though the quietude was favorable to his project, Phariom shivered with a chill of deathly menace and desolation. The hoofs of his camel rang on the pavement with a startling and preternatural clangor, and he thought that the ears of hidden ghouls, listening alertly behind the silence, must surely hear them.

However, there was no stirring of life in that sepulchral gloom. Reaching the shelter of one of the thick groups of ancient cedars, he dismounted and tied the dromedary to a low-growing branch. Keeping among the trees, like a shadow among shadows, he approached the temple with infinite wariness, and circled it slowly, finding that its four doorways, which corresponded to the four quarters of the Earth, were all wide open, deserted, and equally dark. Returning at length to the eastern side, on which he had tethered his camel, he emboldened himself to enter the blackly gaping portal.

Crossing the threshold, he was engulfed instantly by a dead and clammy darkness, touched with the faint fetor of corruption, and a smell as of charred bone and flesh. He thought that he was in a huge corridor, and feeling his way forward along the right-hand wall, he soon came to a sudden turn, and saw a bluish glimmering far ahead, as if in some central adytum where the hall ended. Massy columns were silhouetted against the glimmering; and across it, as he drew nearer, several dark and muffled figures passed, presenting the profiles of enormous skulls. Two of them were sharing the burden of a human body which they carried in their arms. To Phariom, pausing in the shadowy hall, it appeared that the vague taint of putrescence upon the air grew stronger for a few instants after the figure had come and gone.

They were not succeeded by any others, and the fane resumed its mausolean stillness. But the youth waited for many minutes, doubtful and trepidant, before venturing to go on. An oppression of mortuary mystery thickened the air, and stifled him like the noisome effluvia of catacombs. His ears became intolerably acute, and he heard a dim humming, a sound of deep and viscid voices indistinguishably bent, that appeared to issue from crypts beneath the temple.

Stealing at length to the hall's end, he peered beyond into what was obviously the main sanctuary: a low and many-pillared room, whose vastness was but half-revealed by the bluish fires that glowed and flickered in numerous urnlike vessels borne aloft on slender stelae.

Phariom hesitated upon that awful threshold, for the mingled odors of burnt and decaying flesh were heavier on the air, as if he had drawn nearer to their sources; and the thick humming seemed to ascend from a dark stairway in the floor, beside the left-hand wall. But the room, to all appearance, was empty of life, and nothing stirred except the wavering lights and shadows. The watcher discerned the outlines of a vast table in the center, carved from the same black stone as the building itself. Upon the table, half lit by the flaming urns, or shrouded by the umbrage of the heavy columns, a number of people lay side by side; and Phariom knew that he had found the black altar of Mordiggian, whereon were disposed the bodies claimed by the god.

A wild and stifling fear contended with a wilder hope in his bosom. Trembling, he went toward the table; and a cold clamminess, wrought by the presence of the dead, assailed him. The table was nearly thirty feet in length, and it rose waist-high on a dozen mighty legs. Beginning at the nearer end, he passed along the row of corpses, peering fearfully into each upturned face. Both sexes, and many ages and differing ranks were represented. Nobles and rich merchants were crowded by beggars in filthy rags. Some were newly dead, and others, it seemed, had lain there for days, and were beginning to show the marks of corruption. There were many gaps in the ordered row, suggesting that certain of the corpses had been removed. Phariom went on in the dim light, searching for the loved features of Elaith. At last, when he was nearing the further end, and had begun to fear that she was not among them, he found her.

With the cryptic pallor and stillness of her strange malady upon her, she lay unchanged on the chill stone. A great thankfulness was born in the heart of Phariom, for he felt sure that she was not dead — and that she had not awakened at any time to the horrors of the temple. If he could bear her away from the hateful purlieus of Zul-Bha-Sair without detection, she would recover from her death-simulating sickness.

Cursorily, he noted that another woman was lying beside Elaith, and recognized her as the beautiful Arctela, whose bearers he had followed almost to the portals of the fane. He gave her no second glance, but stooped to lift Elaith in his arms.

At that moment, he heard a murmur of low voices in the direction of the door by which he had entered the sanctuary. Thinking that some of the priests had returned, he dropped swiftly on hands and knees and crawled beneath the ponderous table, which afforded the only accessible hiding-place. Retreating into shadow beyond the glimmering shed from the lofty urns, he waited and looked out between the pillar-thick legs.

The voices grew louder, and he saw the curiously sandaled feet and shortish robes of three persons who approached the table of the dead and paused in the very spot where he himself had stood a few instants before. Who they were, he could not surmise; but their garments of light and swarthy red were not the shroudings of Mordiggian's priests. He was uncertain whether or not they had seen him; and crouching in the low space beneath the table, he plucked his dagger from its sheath.

Now, he was able to distinguish three voices, one solemn and unctuously imperative, one somewhat guttural and growling, and the other shrill and nasal. The accents were alien, differing from those of the men of Zul-Bha-Sair, and the words were often strange to Phariom. Also, much of the converse was inaudible.

"... here... at the end," said the solemn voice. "Be swift... We have no time to loiter."

"Yes, Master," came the growling voice. "But who is this other?... Truly, she is very fair."

A discussion seemed to take place, in discreetly lowered tones. Apparently the owner of the guttural voice was urging something that the other two opposed. The listener could distinguish only a word or two here and there; but he gathered that the name of the first person was Vembi-Tsith, and that the one who spoke in a nasal shrilling was called Narghai. At last, above the others, the grave accents of the man addressed only as the Master were clearly audible:

"I do not altogether approve... It will delay our departure... and the two must ride on one dromedary. But take her, Vemba-Tsith, if you can perform the necessary spells unaided. I have no time for a double incantation... It will be a good test of your proficiency."

There was a mumbling as of thanks or acknowledgment from Vemba-Tsith. Then the voice of the Master: "Be quiet now and make haste." To Phariom, wondering vaguely and uneasily as to the import of this colloquy, it seemed that two of the three men pressed closer to the table, as if stooping above the dead. He heard a rustling of cloth upon stone, and an instant later, he saw that all three were departing among the columns and stelae, in a direction opposite to that from which they had entered the sanctuary. Two of them carried burdens that glimmered palely and indistinctly in the shadows.

A black horror clutched at the heart of Phariom, for all too clearly he surmised the nature of those burdens and the possible identity of one of them. Quickly he crawled forth from his hiding-place and saw that Elaith was gone from the black table, together with the girl Arctela. He saw the vanishing of shadowy figures in the gloom that zoned the chamber's western wall. Whether the abductors were ghouls, or worse than ghouls, he could not know, but he followed swiftly, forgetful of all caution in his concern for Elaith.

Reaching the wall, he found the mouth of a corridor, and plunged into it headlong. Somewhere in the gloom ahead, he saw a ruddy glimmering of light. Then he heard a sullen, metallic grating; and the glimmer narrowed to a slit-like gleam, as if the door of the chamber from which it issued were being closed.

Following the blind wall, he came to that slit of crimson light. A door of darkly tarnished bronze had been left ajar, and Phariom peered in on a weird, unholy scene, illumined by the blood-like flames that flared and soared unsteadily from high urns upborne on sable pedestals.

The room was full of a sensuous luxury that accorded strangely with the dull, funereal stone of that temple of death. There were couches and carpets of superbly figured stuffs, vermilion, gold, azure, silver; and jeweled censers of unknown metals stood in the corners. A low table at one side was littered with curious bottles, and occult appliances such as might be used in medicine or sorcery.

Elaith was lying on one of the couches, and near her, on a second couch, the body of the girl Arctela had been disposed. The abductors, whose faces Phariom now beheld for the first time, were busying themselves with singular preparations that mystified him prodigiously. His impulse to invade the room was repressed by a sort of wonder that held him enthralled and motionless.

One of the three, a tall, middle-aged man whom he identified as the Master, had assembled certain peculiar vessels, including a small brazier and a censer, and had set them on the floor beside Arctela. The second, a younger man with lecherously slitted eyes, had placed similar impedimenta before Elaith. The third, who was also young and evil of aspect, merely stood and looked on with an apprehensive, uneasy air.

Phariom divined that the men were sorcerers when, with a deftness born of long practice, they lit the censers and braziers, and began simultaneously the intonation of rhythmically measured words in a strange tongue accompanied by the sprinkling, at regular intervals, of black oils that fell with a great hissing on the coals in the braziers and sent up enormous clouds of pearly smoke. Dark threads of vapor serpentined from the censers, interweaving themselves like veins through the dim, misshapen figures as of ghostly giants that were formed by the lighter fumes. A reek of intolerably acrid balsams filled the chamber, assailing and troubling the senses of Phariom, till the scene wavered before him and took on a dreamlike vastness, a narcotic distortion.

The voices of the necromancers mounted and fell as if in some unholy paean. Imperious, exigent, they seemed to implore the consummation of forbidden blasphemy. Like thronging phantoms, writhing and swirling with malignant life, the vapors rose about the couches on which lay the dead girl and the girl who bore the outward likeness of death.

Then, as the fumes were riven apart in their baleful seething, Phariom saw that the pale figure of Elaith had stirred like a sleeper who awakens, that she had opened her eyes and was lifting a feeble hand from the gorgeous couch. The younger necromancer ceased his chanting on a sharply broken cadence; but the solemn tones of the other still went on, and still there was a spell on the limbs and senses of Phariom, making it impossible for him to stir.

Slowly the vapors thinned like a rout of dissolving phantoms. The watcher saw that the dead girl, Arctela, was rising to her feet like a somnambulist. The chanting of Abnon-Tha, standing before her, came sonorously to an end. In the awful silence that followed, Phariom heard a weak cry from Elaith, and then the jubilant, growling voice of Vemba-Tsith, who was stooping above her:

"Behold, O Abnon-Tha! My spells are swifter than yours, for she that I have chosen awakened before Arctela!"

Phariom was released from his thralldom, as if through the lifting of an evil enchantment. He flung back the ponderous door of darkened bronze, that ground with protesting clangors on its hinges. His dagger drawn, he rushed into the room.

Elaith, her eyes wide with piteous bewilderment, turned toward him and made an ineffectual effort to arise from the couch. Arctela, mute and submissive before Abnon-Tha, appeared to heed nothing but the will of the necromancer. She was like a fair and soulless automaton. The sorcerers, turning as Phariom entered, sprang back with instant agility before his onset, and drew the short, cruelly crooked swords which they all carried. Narghai struck the knife from Phariom's fingers with a darting blow that shattered its thin blade at the hilt, and VembaTsith, his weapon swinging back in a vicious arc, would have killed the youth promptly if Abnon-Tha had not intervened and bade him stay.

Phariom, standing furious but irresolute before the lifted swords, was aware of the darkly searching eyes of Abnon-Tha, like those of some nyctalopic bird of prey.

"I would know the meaning of this intrusion," said the necromancer. "Truly, you are bold to enter the temple of Mordiggian."

"I came to find the girl who lies yonder," declared Phariom. "She is Elaith, my wife, who was claimed unjustly by the god. But tell me, why have you brought her to this room, from the table of Mordiggian, and what manner of men are you, that raise up the dead as you have raised this other woman?"

"I am Abnon-Tha, the necromancer, and these others are my pupils, Narghai and Vemba-Tsith. Give thanks to Vemba-Tsith, for verily he has brought back your wife from the purlieus of the dead with a skill excelling that of his master. She awoke ere the incantation was finished!"

Phariom glared with implacable suspicion at Abnon-Tha. "Elaith was not dead, but only as one in a trance," he averred. "It was not your pupil's sorcery that awakened her. And verily whether Elaith be dead or living is not a matter that should concern any but myself. Permit us to depart, for I wish to remove with her from Zul-Bha-Sair, in which we are only passing travelers."

So speaking, he turned his back on the necromancers, and went over to Elaith, who regarded him with dazed eyes but uttered his name feebly as he clasped her in his arms.

"Now, this is a remarkable coincidence," purred Abnon-Tha. "I and my pupils are also planning to depart from Zul-Bha-Sair, and we start this very night. Perhaps you will honor us with your company."

"I thank you," said Phariom, curtly. "But I am not sure that our roads lie together. Elaith and I would go toward Tasuun."

"Now, by the black altar of Mordiggian, that is still stranger coincidence, for Tasuun is also our destination We take with us the resurrected girl Arctela, whom I have deemed too fair for the charnel god and his ghouls."

Phariom divined the dark evil that lay behind the oily, mocking speeches of the necromancer. Also, he saw the furtive and sinister sign that Abnon-Tha had made to his assistants. Weaponless, he could only give a formal assent to the sardonic proposal. He knew well that he would not be permitted to leave the temple alive, for the narrow eyes of Narghai and Vemba-Tsith, regarding him closely, were alight with the red lust of murder.

"Come," said Abnon-Tha, in a voice of imperious command. "It is time to go." He turned to the still figure of Arctela and spoke an unknown word. With vacant eyes and noctambulistic paces, she followed at his heels as he stepped toward the open door. Phariom had helped Elaith to her feet, and was whispering words of reassurance in an effort to lull the growing horror and confused alarm that he saw in her eyes. She was able to walk, albeit slowly and uncertainly. Vemba-Tsith and Narghai drew back, motioning that she and Phariom should precede them; but Phariom, sensing their intent to slay him as soon as his back was turned, obeyed unwillingly and looked desperately about for something that he could seize as a weapon.

One of the metal braziers, full of smoldering coals, was at his very feet. He stooped quickly, lifted it in his hands, and turned upon the necromancers. Vemba-Tsith, as he had suspected, was prowling toward him with upraised, sword, and was making ready to strike. Phariom hurled the brazier and its glowing contents full in the necromancer's face, and Vemba-Tsith went down with a terrible, smothered cry. Narghai, snarling ferociously, leapt foreward to assail the defenseless youth. His scimitar gleamed with a wicked luster in the lurid glare of the urns as he swung it back for the blow. But the weapon did not fall; and Phariom, steeling himself against the impending death, became aware that Narghai was staring beyond him as if petrified by the vision of some Gorgonian specter.

As if compelled by another will than his own, the youth turned and saw the thing that had halted Narghai's blow. Arctela and Abnon-Tha, pausing before the open door, were outlined against a colossal shadow that was not wrought by anything in the room. It filled the portals from side to side, it towered above the lintel — and then, swiftly, it became more than a shadow: it was a bulk of darkness, black and opaque, that somehow blinded the eyes with a strange dazzlement. It seemed to suck the flame from the red urns and fill the chamber with a chill of utter death and voidness. Its form was that of a worm-shapen column, huge as a dragon, its further coils still issuing from the gloom of the corridor; but it changed from moment to moment, swirling and spinning as if alive with the vortical energies of dark eons. Briefly it took the semblance of some demoniac giant with eyeless head and limbless body; and then, leaping and spreading like smoky fire, it swept forward into the chamber.

Abnon-Tha fell back before it, with frantic mumblings of malediction or exorcism; but Arctela, pale and slight and motionless, remained full in its path, while the thing enfolded her and enveloped her with a hungry flaring until she was hidden wholly from view.

Phariom, supporting Elaith, who leaned weakly on his shoulder as if about to swoon, was powerless to move. He forgot the murderous Narghai, and it seemed that he and Elaith were but faint shadows in the presence of embodied death and dissolution. He saw the blackness grow and wax with the towering of fed flame as it closed about Arctela; and he saw it gleam with eddying hues of somber iris, like the spectrum of a sable sun. For an instant, he heard a soft and flame-like murmuring. Then, quickly and terribly, the thing ebbed from the room. Arctela was gone, as if she had dissolved like a phantom on the air. Borne on a sudden gust of strangely mingled heat and cold, there came an acrid odor, such as would rise from a burnt-out funeral pyre.

"Mordiggian!" shrilled Narghai, in hysteric terror. "It was the god Mordiggian! He has taken Arctela!"

It seemed that his cry was answered by a score of sardonic echoes, unhuman as the howling of hyenas, and yet articulate, that repeated the name Mordiggian. Into the room, from the dark hall, there poured a horde of creatures whose violet robes alone identi-fied them in Phariom's eyes as the priests of the ghoul-god. They had removed the skull-like masks, revealing heads and faces that were half anthropomorphic, half canine, and wholly diabolic. Also, they had taken off the fingerless gloves... There were at least a dozen of them. Their curving talons gleamed in the bloody light like the hooks of darkly tarnished metal; their spiky teeth, longer than coffin nails, protruded from snarling lips. They closed like a ring of jackals on Abnon-Tha and Narghai, driving them back into the far-thest corner. Several others, entering tardily, fell with a bestial ferocity on Vemba-Tsith, who had begun to revive, and was moan-ing and writhing on the floor amid the scattered coals of the brazier.

They seemed to ignore Phariom and Elaith, who stood looking on as if in some baleful trance. But the hindmost, ere he joined the assailants of Vemba-Tsith, turned to the youthful pair and ad-dressed them in a hoarse, hollow voice, like a tomb-reverberate barking:

"Go, for Mordiggian is a just god, who claims only the dead, and has no concern with the living. And we, the priests of Mor-diggian, deal in our own fashion with those who would violate his law by removing the dead from the temple."

Phariom, with Elaith still leaning on his shoulder, went out into the dark hall, hearing a hideous clamor in which the screams of men were mingled with a growling as of jackals, a laughter as of hyenas. The clamor ceased as, they entered the blue-lit sanctuary and passed toward the outer corridor, and the silence that filled Mordiggian's fane behind them was deep as the silence of the dead on the black altar-table.

THE COLOSSUS OF YLOURGNE

I. *The Flight of the Necromancer*

The thrice-infamous Nathaire, alchemist, astrologer and necromancer, with his ten devil-given pupils, had departed very suddenly and under circumstances of strict secrecy from the town of Vyones. It was widely thought, among the people of that vicinage, that his departure had been prompted by a salutary fear of ecclesiastical thumbscrews and faggots. Other wizards, less notorious than he, had already gone to the stake during a year of unusual inquisitory zeal; and it was well-known that Nathaire had incurred the reprobation of the Church. Few, therefore, considered the reason of his going a mystery; but the means of transit which he had employed, as well as the destination of the sorcerer and his pupils, were regarded as more than problematic.

A thousand dark and superstitious rumours were abroad; and passers made the sign of the Cross when they neared the tall, gloomy house which Nathaire had built in blasphemous proximity to the great cathedral and had filled with a furniture of Satanic luxury and strangeness. Two daring thieves, who had entered the mansion when the fact of its desertion became well established, reported that much of this furniture, as well as the books and other paraphernalia of Nathaire, had seemingly departed with its owner, doubtless to the same fiery bourn. This served to augment the unholy mystery: for it was patently impossible that Nathaire and his ten apprentices, with several cart-loads of household belongings, could have passed the ever-guarded city gates in any legitimate manner without the knowledge of the custodians.

It was said by the more devout and religious moiety that the Archfiend, with a legion of bat-winged assistants, had borne them away bodily at moonless midnight. There were clerics, and also reputable burghers, who professed to have seen the flight of man-like shapes upon the blotted stars together with others that were not men, and to have heard the wailing cries of the hell-bound crew as they passed in an evil cloud over the roofs and city walls.

Others believed that the sorcerers had transported themselves from Vyones through their own diabolic arts, and had withdrawn to some unfrequented fastness where Nathaire, who had long been in feeble health, could hope to die in such peace and serenity as might be enjoyed by one who stood between the flames of the auto-da-fé and those of Abaddon. It was thought that he had lately cast his own horoscope, for the first time in his fifty-odd years, and had read therein an impending conjunction of disastrous planets, signifying early death.

Others still, among whom were certain rival astrologers and enchanters, said that Nathaire had retired from the public view merely that he might commune without interruption with various coadjutive demons; and thus might weave, unmolested, the black spells of a supreme and lycanthropic malice. These spells, they hinted, would in due time be visited upon Vyones and perhaps upon the entire region of Averoigne; and would no doubt take the form of a fearsome pestilence, or a wholesale invultuation, or a realm-wide incursion of succubi and incubi.

Amid the seething of strange rumours, many half-forgotten tales were recalled, and new legends were created overnight Much was made of the obscure nativity of Nathaire and his dubitable wanderings before he had settled, six years previous, in Vyones. People said that he was fiend-begotten, like the fabled Merlin: his father being no less a personage than Alastor, demon of revenge; and his mother a deformed and dwarfish sorceress. From the former, he had taken his spitefulness and malignity; from the latter, his squat, puny physique.

He had travelled in Orient lands, and had learned from Egyptian or Saracenic masters the unhallowed art of necromancy, in whose practice he was unrivalled. There were black whispers anent the use he had made of long-dead bodies, of fleshless bones, and the service he had wrung from buried men that the angel of doom alone could lawfully raise up. He had never been popular, though many had sought his advice and assistance in the furthering of their own more or less dubious affairs. Once, in the third year after his coming to Vyones, he had been stoned in public because of his bruited necromancies, and had been permanently lamed by a well-directed cobble. This injury, it was thought, he had never forgiven; and he was said to return the antagonism of the clergy with the hellish hatred of an Antichrist.

Apart from the sorcerous evils and abuses of which he was commonly suspected, he had long been looked upon as a corrupter of youth. Despite his minikin stature, his deformity and ugliness, he possessed a remarkable power, a mesmeric persuasion; and his pupils, whom he was said to have plunged into bottomless and ghoulish iniquities, were young men of the most brilliant promise. On the whole, his vanishment was regarded as a quite providential riddance.

Among the people of the city there was one man who took no part in the sombre gossip and lurid speculation. This man was Gaspard du Nord, himself a student of the proscribed sciences, who had been numbered for a year among the pupils of Nathaire but had chosen to withdraw quietly from the master's household after learning the enormities that would attend his further initiation. He had, however, taken with him much rare and peculiar knowledge, together with a certain insight into the baleful powers and night-dark motives of the necromancer.

Because of this knowledge and insight, Gaspard preferred to remain silent when he heard of Nathaire's departure. Also, he did not think it well to revive the memory of his own past pupilage. Alone with his books, in a sparsely furnished attic, he frowned above a small, oblong mirror, framed with an arabesque of golden vipers, that had once been the property of Nathaire.

It was not the reflection of his own comely and youthful though subtly lined face that caused him to frown. Indeed, the mirror was of another kind than that which reflects the features of the gazer. In its depths, for a few instants, he had beheld a strange and ominous-looking scene, whose participants were known to him but whose location he could not recognize or orientate. Before he could study it closely, the mirror had clouded as if with the rising of alchemic fumes, and he had seen no more.

This clouding, he reflected, could mean only one thing: Nathaire had known himself watched and had put forth a counterspell that rendered the clairvoyant mirror useless. It was the realization of this fact, together with the brief, sinister glimpse of Nathaire's present activities, that troubled Gaspard and caused a chill horror to mount slowly in his mind: a horror that had not yet found a palpable form or a name.

2. The Gathering of the Dead

The departure of Nathaire and his pupils occurred in the late spring of 1281, during the interlunar dark. Afterwards a new moon waxed above the flowery fields and bright-leafed woods and waned in ghostly silver. With its waning, people began to talk of other magicians and fresher mysteries.

Then, in the moon-deserted nights of early summer, there came a series of disappearances far more unnatural and inexplicable than that of the dwarfish, malignant sorcerer.

It was found one day, by grave-diggers who had gone early to their toil in a cemetery outside the walls of Vyones, that no less than six newly occupied graves had been opened, and the bodies, which were those of reputable citizens, removed. On closer examination, it became all too evident that this removal had not been effected by robbers. The coffins, which lay aslant or stood protruding upright from the mould, offered all the appearance of having been shattered from within as if by the use of extrahuman strength; and the fresh earth itself was upheaved, as if the dead men, in some awful, untimely resurrection, had actually dug their way to the surface.

The corpses had vanished utterly, as if hell had swallowed them; and, as far as could be learned, there were no eyewitnesses of their fate. In those devil-ridden times, only one explanation of the happening seemed credible: demons had entered the graves and had taken bodily possession of the dead, compelling them to arise and go forth.

To the dismay and horror of all Averoigne, the strange vanishment was followed with appalling promptness by many others of a like sort. It seemed as if an occult, resistless summons had been laid upon the dead. Nightly, for a period of two weeks, the cemeteries of Vyones and also those of other towns, of villages and hamlets, gave up a ghastly quota of their tenants. From brazen bolted tombs, from common charnels, from shallow, unconsecrated trenches, from the marble lidded vaults of churches and cathedrals, the weird exodus went on without cessation.

Worse than this, if possible, there were newly ceremented corpses that leapt from their biers or catafalques, and disregarding the horrified watchers, ran with great bounds of automatic frenzy into the night, never to be seen again by those who lamented them.

In every case, the missing bodies were those of young stalwart men who had died but recently and had met their death through violence or accident rather than wasting illness. Some were criminals who had paid the penalty of their misdeeds; others were men-at-arms or constables, slain in the execution of their duty. Knights who had died in tourney or personal combat were numbered among them; and many were the victims of the robber bands who infested Averoigne at that time. There were monks, merchants, nobles, yeomen, pages, priests; but none, in any case, who had passed the prime of life. The old and infirm, it seemed, were safe from the animating demons.

The situation was looked upon by the more superstitious as a veritable omening of the world's end. Satan was making war with his cohorts and was carrying the bodies of the holy dead into hellish captivity. The consternation increased a hundredfold when it became plain that even the most liberal sprinkling of holy water, the performance of the most awful and cogent exorcisms, failed utterly to give protection against this diabolic ravishment. The Church owned itself powerless to cope with the strange evil; and the forces of secular law could do nothing to arraign or punish the intangible agency.

Because of the universal fear that prevailed, no effort was made to follow the missing cadavers. Ghastly tales, however, were told by late wayfarers who had met certain of these liches, striding alone or in companies along the roads of Averoigne. They gave the appearance of being deaf, dumb, totally insensate, and of hurrying with horrible speed and sureness towards a remote, predestined goal. The general direction of their flight, it seemed, was eastward; but only with the cessation of the exodus, which had numbered several hundred people, did any one begin to suspect the actual destination of the dead.

This destination, it somehow became rumoured, was the ruinous castle of Ylourgne, beyond the werewolf-haunted forest, in the outlying, semi-mountainous hills of Averoigne.

Ylourgne, a great, craggy pile that had been built by a line of evil and marauding barons now extinct, was a place that even the goatherds preferred to shun. The wrathful spectres of its bloody lords were said to move turbulently in its crumbling halls; and its chatelaines were the Undead. No one cared to dwell in the shadow of its cliff-founded walls; and the nearest abode of living men was a small Cistercian monastery, more than a mile away on the opposite slope of the valley.

The monks of this austere brotherhood held little commerce with the world beyond the hills; and few were the visitors who sought admission at their high-perched portals. But, during that dreadful summer, following the disappearances of the dead, a weird and disquieting tale went forth from the monastery throughout Averoigne.

Beginning with late spring, the Cistercian monks were compelled to take cognizance of sundry odd phenomena in the old, long-deserted ruins of Ylourgne, which were visible from their windows, They had beheld flaring lights, where lights should not have been: flames of uncanny blue and crimson that shuddered behind the broken, weed-grown embrasures or rose starwards above the jagged crenelations. Hideous noises had issued from the ruin by night together with the flames; and the monks had heard a clangour as of hellish anvils and hammers, a ringing of gigantic armour and maces, and had deemed that Ylourgne was become a mustering-ground of devils. Mephitic odours as of brimstone and burning flesh had floated across the valley; and even by day, when the noises were silent and the lights no longer flared, a thin haze of hell-blue vapour hung upon the battlements. It was plain, the monks thought, that the place had been occupied from beneath by subterrestrial beings; for no one was seen to approach it by way of the bare, open slopes and crags. Observing these signs of the Arch-foe's activity in their neighbourhood, they crossed themselves with new fervour and frequency, and said their Paters and Aves more interminably than before. Their toil and austerities, also, they re-doubled. Otherwise, since the old castle was a place abandoned by men, they took no heed of the supposed occupation, deeming it well to mind their own affairs unless in case of overt Satanic hostility.

They kept a careful watch; but for several weeks they saw no one who actually entered Ylourgne or emerged therefrom. Except for the nocturnal lights and noises, and the hovering vapour by day, there was no proof of tenantry either human or diabolic. Then, one morning, in the valley below the terraced gardens of the monastery, two brothers, hoeing weeds in a carrot-patch, beheld the passing of a singular train of people who came from the direction of the great forest of Averoigne and went upwards climbing the steep, chasmy slope towards Ylourgne.

These people, the monks averred, were striding along in great haste, with stiff but flying steps; and all were strangely pale of fea-ture and were habited in the garments of the grave. The shrouds of some were torn and ragged; and all were dusty with travel or grimed with the mould of interment. The people numbered a dozen or more; and after them, at intervals, there came several stragglers, attired like the rest. With marvellous agility and speed, they mounted the hill and disappeared at length amid the lowering walls of Ylourgne.

At this time, no rumour of the ravished graves and biers had reached the Cistercians. The tale was brought to them later, after they had beheld, on many successive mornings, the passing of small or great companies of the dead towards the devil-taken castle. Hun-dreds of these liches, they swore, had filed by beneath the monas-tery; and doubtless many others had gone past unnoted in the dark. None, however, were seen to come forth from Ylourgne, which had swallowed them up like the undisgorging Pit.

Though direly frightened and sorely scandalized, the brothers still thought it well to refrain from action. Some, the hardiest, irked by all these flagrant signs of evil, had desired to visit the ruins with holy water and lifted crucifixes, But their abbot, in his wisdom, enjoined them to wait. In the meanwhile, the nocturnal flames grew brighter, the noises louder.

Also, in the course of this waiting, while incessant prayers went up from the little monastery, a frightful thing occurred. One of the brothers, a stout fellow named Theophile, in violation of the rigorous discipline, had made over-frequent visits to the wine-casks. No doubt he had tried to drown his pious horror at these untoward happenings, At any rate, after his potations, he had the ill-luck to wander out among the precipices and break his neck.

Sorrowing for his death and dereliction, the brothers laid Theophile in the chapel and chanted their masses for his soul. These masses, in the dark hours before morning, were interrupted by the untimely resurrection of the dead monk, who, with his head lolling horribly on his broken neck, rushed as if fiend-ridden from the chapel and ran down the hill towards the demon flames and clamours of Ylourgne.

3. *The Testimony of the Monks*

Following the above-related occurrence, two of the brothers who had previously desired to visit the haunted castle again applied to the abbot for this permission, saying that God would surely aid them in avenging the abduction of Theophile's body as well as the taking of many others from consecrated ground. Marvelling at the hardihood of these lusty monks, who preposed to beard the Arch-enemy in his lair, the abbot permitted them to go forth, furnished with aspergilluses and flasks of holy water, and bearing great crosses of hornbeam, such as would have served for maces with which to brain an armoured knight.

The monks, whose names were Bernard and Stephane, went boldly up at middle forenoon to assail the evil stronghold. It was an arduous climb, among overhanging boulders and along slippery scarps; but both were stout and agile, and, moreover, well accustomed to such climbing. Since the day was sultry and airless, their white robes were soon stained with sweat; but pausing only for brief prayer, they pressed on; and in good season they neared the castle, upon whose grey, time-eroded ramparts they could still descry no evidence of occupation or activity.

The deep moat that had once surrounded the place was now dry, and had been partly filled by crumbling earth and detritus from the walls. The drawbridge had rotted away; but the blocks of the barbican, collapsing into the moat, had made a sort of rough causey on which it was possible to cross. Not without trepidation, and lifting their crucifixes as warriors lift their weapons in the escalade of an armed fortress, the brothers climbed over the ruin of the barbican into the courtyard.

This too, like the battlements, was seemingly deserted. Overgrown nettles, rank grasses and sapling trees were rooted between its paving-stones. The high, massive donjon, the chapel, and that portion of the castellated structure containing the great hall, had preserved their main outlines after centuries of dilapidation. To the left of the broad bailey, a doorway yawned like the mouth of a dark cavern in the cliffy mass of the hall-building; and from this doorway there issued a thin, bluish vapour, writhing in phantom coils towards the unclouded heavens.

Approaching the doorway, the brothers beheld a gleaming of red fires within, like the eyes of dragons blinking through infernal murk. They felt sure that the place was an outpost of Erebus, an ante-chamber of the Pit; but nevertheless, they entered bravely, chanting loud exorcisms and brandishing their mighty crosses of hornbeam.

Passing through the cavernous doorway, they could see but indistinctly in the gloom, being somewhat blinded by the summer sunlight they had left. Then, with the gradual clearing of their vision, a monstrous scene was limned before them, with ever-growing details of crowding horror and grotesquery. Some of the details were obscure and mysteriously terrifying; others, all too plain, were branded as if with sudden, ineffaceable hell-fire on the minds of the monks.

They stood on the threshold of a colossal chamber, which seemed to have been made by the tearing down of upper floors and inner partitions adjacent to the castle hall, itself a room of huge extent. The chamber seemed to recede through interminable shadow, shafted with sunlight falling through the rents of ruin: sunlight that was powerless to dissipate the infernal gloom and mystery.

The monks averred later that they saw many people moving about the place, together with sundry demons, some of whom were shadowy and gigantic, and others barely to be distinguished from the men. These people, as well as their familiars, were occupied with the tending of reverberatory furnaces and immense pear-shaped and gourd-shaped vessels such as were used in alchemy. Some, also, were stooping above great fuming cauldrons, like sorcerers, busy with the brewing of terrible drugs. Against the opposite wall, there were two enormous vats, built of stone and mortar, whose circular sides rose higher than a man's head, so that Bernard and Stephane were unable to determine their contents. One of the vats gave forth a whitish glimmering; the other, a ruddy luminosity.

Near the vats, and somewhat between them, there stood a sort of low couch or litter, made of luxurious, weirdly figured fabrics such as the Saracens weave. On this the monks discerned a dwarfish being, pale and wizened, with eyes of chill flame that shone like evil beryls through the dusk. The dwarf, who had all the air of a feeble moribund, was supervising the toils of the men and their familiars.

The dazed eyes of the brothers began to comprehend other details. They saw that several corpses, among which they recognized that of Theophile, were lying on the middle floor, together with a heap of human bones that had been wrenched asunder at the joints, and great lumps of flesh piled like the carvings of butchers. One of the men was lifting the bones and dropping them into a cauldron beneath which there glowed a rubycoloured fire; and another was flinging the lumps of flesh into a tub filled with some hueless liquid that gave forth an evil hissing as of a thousand serpents.

Others had stripped the grave-clothes from one of the cadavers, and were starting to assail it with long knives. Others still were mounting rude flights of stone stairs along the walls of the immense vats, carrying vessels filled with semi-liquescent matters which they emptied over the high rims.

Appalled at this vision of human and Satanic turpitude, and feeling a more than righteous indignation, the monks resumed their chanting of sonorous exorcisms and rushed forward. Their entrance, it appeared, was not perceived by the heinously occupied crew of sorcerers and devils.

Bernard and Stephane, filled with an ardour of godly wrath, were about to fling themselves upon the butchers who had started to assail the dead body. This corpse they recognized as being that of a notorious outlaw, named Jacques Le Loupgarou, who had been slain a few days previous in combat with the officers of the state. Le Loupgarou, noted for his brawn, his cunning and his ferocity, had long terrorized the woods and highways of Averoigne. His great body had been half eviscerated by the swords of the constabulary; and his beard was stiff and purple with the dried blood of a ghastly wound that had cloven his face from temple to mouth. He had died unshriven, but nevertheless, the monks were unwilling to see his helpless cadaver put to some unhallowed use beyond the surmise of Christians.

The pale, malignant-looking dwarf had now perceived the brothers. They heard him cry out in a shrill, imperatory tone that rose above the ominous hiss of the cauldrons and the hoarse mutter of men and demons.

They knew not his words, which were those of some outlandish tongue and sounded like an incantation. Instantly, as if in response to an order, two of the men turned from their unholy chemistry, and lifting copper basins filled with an unknown, fetid liquor, hurled the contents of these vessels in the faces of Bernard and Stephane.

The brothers were blinded by the stinging fluid, which bit their flesh as with many serpents' teeth; and they were overcome by the noxious fumes, so that their great crosses dropped from their hands and they both fell unconscious on the castle floor.

Recovering anon their sight and their other senses, they found that their hands had been tied with heavy thongs of gut, so that they were now helpless and could no longer wield their crucifixes or the sprinklers of holy water which they carried.

In this ignominious condition, they heard the voice of the evil dwarf, commanding them to arise. They obeyed, though clumsily and with difficulty, being denied the assistance of their hands. Bernard, who was still sick with the poisonous vapour he had inhaled, fell twice before he succeeded in standing erect; and his discomfiture was greeted with a cachinnation of foul, obscene laughter from the assembled sorcerers.

Now, standing, the monks were taunted by the dwarf, who mocked and reviled them, with appalling blasphemies such as could be uttered only by a bond-servant of Satan. At last, according to their sworn testimony, he said to them:

"Return to your kennel, ye whelps of Ialdabaoth, and take with you this message: They that came here as many shall go forth as one."

Then, in obedience to a dreadful formula spoken by the dwarf, two of the familiars, who had the shape of enormous and shadowy beasts, approached the body of Le Loupgarou and that of Brother Theophile. One of the foul demons, like a vapour that sinks into a marsh, entered the bloody nostrils of Le Loupgarou, disappearing inch by inch, till its horned and bestial head was withdrawn from sight. The other, in like manner, went in through the nostrils of Brother Theophile, whose head lay weird athwart his shoulder on the broken neck.

Then, when the demons had completed their possession, the bodies, in a fashion horrible to behold, were raised up from the castle floor, the one with ravelled entrails hanging from its wide wounds, the other with a head that dropped forward loosely on its bosom. Then, animated by their devils, the cadavers took up the crosses of hornbeam that had been dropped by Stephane and Bernard; and using the crosses for bludgeons, they drove the monks in ignominious flight from the castle, amid a loud, tempestuous howling of infernal laughter from the dwarf and his necromantic crew. And the nude corpse of Le Loupgarou and the robed cadaver of Theophile followed them far on the chasm-riven slopes below Ylourgne, striking great blows with the crosses, so that the backs of the two Cistercians were become a mass of bloody bruises.

After a defeat so signal and crushing, no more of the monks were emboldened to go up against Ylourgne. The whole monastery, thereafter, devoted itself to triple austerities, to quadrupled prayers; and awaiting the unknown will of God, and the equally obscure machinations of the Devil, maintained a pious faith that was somewhat tempered with trepidation.

In time, through goatherds who visited the monks, the tale of Stephane and Bernard went forth throughout Averoigne, adding to the grievous alarm that had been caused by the wholesale disappearance of the dead. No one knew what was really going on in the haunted castle or what disposition had been made of the hundreds of migratory corpses; for the light thrown on their fate by the monks' story, though lurid and frightful, was all too inconclusive; and the message sent by the dwarf was somewhat cabalistic.

Everyone felt, however, that some gigantic menace, some black, infernal enchantment, was being brewed within the ruinous walls. The malign, moribund dwarf was all too readily identified with the missing sorcerer, Nathaire; and his underlings, it was plain, were Nathaire's pupils.

4. *The Going-Forth of Gaspard du Nord*

Alone in his attic chamber, Gaspard du Nord, student of alchemy and sorcery and quondam pupil of Nathaire, sought repeatedly, but always in vain, to consult the viper-circled mirror. The glass remained obscure and cloudy, as with the risen fumes of Satanical alembics or baleful necromantic braziers. Haggard and weary with long nights of watching, Gaspard knew that Nathaire was even more vigilant than he.

Reading with anxious care the general configuration of the stars, he found the foretokening of a great evil that was to come upon Averoigne. But the nature of the evil was not clearly shown.

In the meanwhile the hideous resurrection and migration of the dead was taking place. All Averoigne shuddered at the manifold enormity. Like the timeless night of a Memphian plague, terror settled everywhere; and people spoke of each new atrocity in bated whispers, without daring to voice the execrable tale aloud. To Gaspard, as to everyone, the whispers came; and likewise, after the horror had apparently ceased in early midsummer, there came the appalling story of the Cistercian monks.

Now, at last, the long-baffled watcher found an inkling of that which he sought. The hiding-place of the fugitive necromancer and his apprentices, at least, had been uncovered; and the disappearing dead were clearly traced to their bourn. But still, even for the per-cipient Gaspard, there remained an undeclared enigma: the exact nature of the abominable brew, the hell-dark sorcery, that Nathaire was concocting in his remote den. Gaspard felt sure of one thing only: the dying, splenetic dwarf, knowing that his allotted time was short, and hating the people of Averoigne with a bottomless ran-cour, would prepare an enormous and maleficent magic without parallel.

Even with his knowledge of Nathaire's proclivities, and his awareness of the well-nigh inexhaustible arcanic science, the reserves of pit-deep wizardry possessed by the dwarf, he could form only vague, terrific conjectures anent the incubated evil. But, as time went on, he felt an ever-deepening oppression, the adumbra-tion of a monstrous menace crawling from the dark rim of the world. He could not shake off his disquietude; and finally he resolved despite the obvious perils of such an excursion, to pay a secret visit to the neightborhood of Ylourgne.

Gaspard, though he came of a well-to-do family, was at that time in straitened circumstances; for his devotion to a somewhat doubtful science had been disapproved by his father. His sole income was a small pittance, purveyed secretly to the youth by his mother and sister. This sufficed for his meagre food, the rent of his room, and a few books and instruments and chemicals; but it would not permit the purchase of a horse or even a humble mule for the proposed journey of more than forty miles.

Undaunted, he set forth on foot, carrying only a dagger and a wallet of food. He timed his wanderings so that he would reach Ylourgne at nightfall in the rising of a full moon. Much of his journey lay through the great, lowering forest, which approached the very walls of Vyones on the eastern side and ran in a sombre arc through Averoigne to the mouth of the rocky valley below Ylourgne. After a few miles, he emerged from the mighty wood of pines and oaks and larches; and thenceforward, for the first day, followed the river Isoile thiough an open, well-peopled plain. He spent the warm summer night beneath a beech-tree, in the vicinity of a small village, not caring to sleep in the lonely woods where robbers and wolves — and creatures of a more baleful repute — were commonly supposed to dwell.

At evening of the second day, after passing through the wildest and oldest portion of the immemorial wood, he came to the steep, stony valley that led to his destination. This valley was the fountainhead of the Isoile, which had dwindled to a mere rivulet. In the brown twilight, between sunset and moonrise, he saw the lights of the Cistercian monastery; and opposite, on the piled, forbidding scarps, the grim and rugged mass of the ruinous stronghold of Ylourgne, with wan and wizard fires flickering behind its high embrasures. Apart from these fires, there was no sign of occupation; and he did not hear at any time the dismal noises reported by the monks.

Gaspard waited till the round moon, yellow as the eye of some immense nocturnal bird, had begun to peer above the darkling valley. Then, very cautiously, since the neighbourhood was strange to him, he started to make his way towards the sombre, brooding castle.

Even for one well-used to such climbing, the escalade would have offered enough difficulty and danger by moonlight. Several times, finding himself at the bottom of a sheer cliff, he was compelled to retrace his hard-won progress; and often he was saved from falling only by stunted shrubs and briars that had taken root in the niggard soil. Breathless, with torn raiment and scored and bleeding hands, he gained at length the shoulder of the craggy height, below the walls.

Here he paused to recover breath and recuperate his flagging strength. He could see from his vantage the pale reflection as of hidden flames, that beat upwards on the inner walls of the high-built donjon. He heard a low hum of confused noises, whose distance and direction were alike baffling. Sometimes they seemed to float downwards from the black battlements, sometimes to issue from subterranean depths far in the hill.

Apart from this remote, ambiguous hum, the night was locked in a mortal stillness. The very winds appeared to shun the vicinity of the dread castle. An unseen, clammy cloud of paralyzing evil hung removeless upon all things; and the pale, swollen moon, the patroness of witches and sorcerers, distilled her green poison above the crumbling towers in a silence older than time.

Gaspard felt the obscenely clinging weight of a more burdenous thing than his own fatigue when he resumed his progress towards the barbican. Invisible webs of the waiting, ever-gathering evil seemed to impede him. The slow, noisome flapping of intangible wings was heavy in his face. He seemed to breathe a surging wind from unfathomable vaults and caverns of corruption. Inaudible howlings, derisive or minatory, thronged in his ears, and foul hands appeared to thrust him back. But, bowing his head as if against a blowing gale, he went on and climbed the mounded ruin of the barbican, into the weedy courtyard.

The place was deserted, to all seeming; and much of it was still deep in the shadows of the walls and turrets. Near by, in the black, silver-crenellated pile, Gaspard saw the open, cavernous doorway described by the monks. It was lit from within by a lurid glare, wannish and eerie as marsh-fires. The humming noise, now audible as a muttering of voices, issued from the doorway; and Gaspard thought that he could see dark, sooty figures moving rapidly in the lit interior.

Keeping in the farther shadows, he stole along the courtyard, making a sort of circuit amid the ruins. He did not dare to approach the open entrance for fear of being seen; though, as far as he could tell, the place was unguarded.

He came to the donjon, on whose upper wall the wan light flickered obliquely through a sort of rift in the long building adjacent. This opening was at some distance from the ground; and Gaspard saw that it had been formerly the door to a stony balcony. A flight of broken steps led upwards along the wall to the half-crumbled remnant of this balcony; and it occurred to the youth that he might climb the steps and peer unobserved into the interior of Ylourgne.

Some of the stairs were missing; and all were in heavy shadow. Gaspard found his way precariously to the balcony, pausing once in considerable alarm when a fragment of the worn stone, loosened by his footfall, dropped with a loud clattering on the courtyard flags below. Apparently it was unheard by the occupants of the castle; and after a little he resumed his climbing.

Cautiously he neared the large, ragged opening through which the light poured upwards. Crouching on a narrow ledge, which was all that remained of the balcony, he peered in on a most astounding and terrific spectacle, whose details were so bewildering that he could barely comprehend their import till after many minutes.

It was plain that the story told by the monks — allowing for their religious bias — had been far from extravagant. Almost the whole interior of the half-ruined pile had been torn down and dismantled to afford room for the activities of Nathaire. This demolition in itself was a superhuman task for whose execution the sorcerer must have employed a legion of familiars as well as his ten pupils.

The vast chamber was fitfully illumed by the glare of athanors and braziers; and, above all, by the weird glimmering from the huge stone vats. Even from his high vantage, the watcher could not see the contents of these vats; but a white luminosity poured, upwards from the rim of one of them, and a flesh-tinted phosphorescence from the other.

Gaspard had seen certain of the experiments and evocations of Nathaire, and was all too familiar with the appurtenances of the dark arts. Within certain limits, he was not squeamish; nor was it likely that he would have been terrified overmuch by the shadowy, uncouth shapes of demons who toiled in the pit below him side by side with the blackclad pupils of the sorcerer. But a cold horror clutched his heart when he saw the incredible, enormous thing that occupied the central floor: the colossal human skeleton a hundred feet in length, stretching for more than the extent of the old castle hall; the skeleton whose bony right foot the group of men and devils, to all appearance, were busily clothing with human flesh!

The prodigious and macabre framework, complete in every part, with ribs like arches of some Satanic nave, shone as if it were still heated by the fires of an infernal welding. It seemed to shimmer and burn with unnatural life, to quiver with malign disquietude in the flickering glare and gloom. The great fingerbones, curving claw-like on the floor, appeared as if they were about to close upon some helpless prey. The tremendous teeth were set in an everlasting grin of sardonic cruelty and malice. The hollow eye-sockets, deep as Tartarean wells, appeared to seethe with myriad, mocking lights, like the eyes of elementals swimming upwards in obscene shadow.

Gaspard was stunned by the shocking and stupendous fantasmagoria that yawned before him like a peopled hell. Afterwards he was never wholly sure of certain things, and could remember very little of the actual manner in which the work of the men and their assistants was being carried on. Dim, dubious, bat-like creatures seemed to be flitting to and fro between one of the stone vats and the group that toiled like sculptors, clothing the bony foot with a reddish plasm which they applied and moulded like so much clay. Gaspard thought, but was not certain later, that this plasm, which gleamed as if with mingled blood and fire, was being brought from the rosy-litten vat in vessels borne by the claws of the shadowy flying creatures. None of them, however, approached the other vat, whose wannish light was momently enfeebled, as if it were dying down.

He looked for the minikin figure of Nathaire, whom he could

not distinguish in the crowded scene. The sick necromancer — if he had not already succumbed to the little-known disease that had long wasted him like an inward flame — was no doubt hidden from view by the colossal skeleton and was perhaps directing the labours of the men and demons from his couch.

Spellbound on that precarious ledge, the watcher failed to hear the furtive, cat-like feet that were climbing behind him on the ruinous stairs. Too late, he heard the clink of a loose fragment close upon his heels; and turning in startlement, he toppled into sheer oblivion beneath the impact of a cudgel-like blow, and did not even know that the beginning fall of his body towards the courtyard had been arrested by his assailant's arms.

5. *The Horror of Ylourgne*

Gaspard, returning from his dark plunge into Lethean emptiness, found himself gazing into the eyes of Nathaire: those eyes of liquid night and ebony, in which swam the chill, malignant fires of stars that had gone down to irremeable perdition. For some time, in the confusion of his senses, he could see nothing but the eyes, which seemed to have drawn him forth like baleful magnets from his swoon. Apparently disembodied, or set in a face too vast for human cognizance, they burned before him in chaotic murk; Then, by degrees, he saw the other features of the sorcerer, and the details of a lurid scene; and became aware of his own situation.

Trying to lift his hands to his aching head, he found that they were bound tightly together at the wrists. He was half lying, half leaning against an object with hard planes and edges that irked his back. This object he discovered to be a sort of alchemic furnace, or athanor, part of a litter of disused apparatus that stood or lay on the castle floor. Cupels, aludels, cucurbits, like enormous gourds and globes, were mingled in strange confusion with the piled, iron-clasped books and the sooty cauldrons and braziers of a darker science.

Nathaire, propped among Saracenic cushions with arabesques of sullen gold and fulgurant scarlet, was peering upon him from a kind of improvised-couch, made with bales of Orient rugs and arrases, to whose luxury the rude walls of the castle, stained with mould and mottled with dead fungi, offered a grotesque foil. Dim lights and evilly swooping shadows flickered across the scene; and Gaspard could hear a guttural hum of voices behind him. Twisting his head a little, he saw one of the stone vats, whose rosy luminosity was blurred and blotted by vampire wings that went to and fro.

"Welcome," said Nathaire, after an interval in which the student began to perceive the fatal progress of illness in the painpinched features before him. "So Gaspard du Nord has come to see his former master!" The harsh, imperatory voice, with demoniac volume, issued appallingly from the wizened frame.

"I have come," said Gaspard, in laconic echo. "Tell me, what devil's work is this in which I find you engaged? And what have you done with the dead bodies that were stolen by your accursed familiars?"

The frail, dying body of Nathaire, as if possessed by some sardonic fiend, rocked to and fro on the luxurious couch in a long, violent gust of laughter, without other reply.

"If your looks bear creditable witness," said Gaspard, when the baleful laughter had ceased, "you are mortally ill, and the time is short in which you can hope to atone for your deeds of malice and make your peace with God — if indeed it still be possible for you to make peace. What foul and monstrous brew are you preparing, to ensure the ultimate perdition of your soul?"

The dwarf was again seized by a spasm of diabolic mirth.

"Nay, nay, my good Gaspard," he said finally. "I have made another bond than the one with which puling cowards try to purchase the good will and forgiveness of the heavenly Tyrant. Hell may take me in the end, if it will; but Hell has paid, and will still pay, an ample and goodly price. I must die soon, it is true, for my doom is written in the stars: but in death, by the grace of Satan, I live again, and shall go forth endowed with the mighty thews of the Anakim, to visit vengeance on the people of Averoigne, who have long hated me for my necromantic wisdom and have held me in derision for my dwarf stature."

"What madness is this whereof you dream?" asked the youth, appalled by the more than human frenzy and malignity that seemed to dilate the shrunken frame of Nathaire and stream in Tartarean lustre from his eyes.

"It is no madness, but a veritable thing: a miracle, mayhap, as life itself is a miracle.... From the fresh bodies of the dead, which otherwise would have rotted away in charnel foulness, my pupils and familiars are making for me, beneath my instruction, the giant form whose skeleton you have beheld. My soul, at the death of its present body, will pass into this colossal tenement through the working of certain spells of transmigration in which my faithful assistants have also been carefully instructed."

"If you had remained with me, Gaspard, and had not drawn back in your petty, pious squeamishness from the marvels and profunditities that I should have unveiled for you, it would now be your privilege to share in the creation of this prodigy.... And if you had come to Ylourgne a little sooner in your presumptuous prying, I might have made a certain use of your stout bones and muscles... the same use I have made of other young men, who died through accident or violence. But it is too late even for this, since the building of the bones has been completed, and it remains only to invest them with human flesh. My good Gaspard, there is nothing whatever to be done with you — except to put you safely out of the way. Providentially, for this purpose, there is an oubliette beneath the castle: a somewhat dismal lodging-place, no doubt, but one that was made strong and deep by the grim lords of Ylourgne."

Gaspard was unable to frame any reply to this sinister and extraordinary speech. Searching his horror-frozen brain for words, he felt himself seized from behind by the hands of unseen beings who had come, no doubt, in answer to some gesture of Nathaire: a gesture which the captive had not perceived. He was blindfolded with some heavy fabric, mouldy and musty as a gravecloth, and was led stumbling through the litter of strange apparatus, and down a winding flight of ruinous, narrow stairs from which the noisome breath of stagnating water, mingled with the oily muskiness of serpents, arose to meet him.

He appeared to descend for a distance that would admit of no return. Slowly the stench grew stronger, more insupportable; the stairs ended; a door clanged sullenly on rusty hinges; and Gaspard was thrust forward on a damp, uneven floor that seemed to have been worn away by myriad feet.

He heard the grating of a ponderous slab of stone. His wrists were untied, the bandage was removed from his eyes, and he saw by the light of flickering torches a round hole that yawned in the oozing floor at his feet. Beside it was the lifted slab that had formed its lid. Before he could turn to see the faces of his captors, to learn if they were men or devils, he was seized rudely and thrust into the gaping hole, He fell through Erebus-like darkness, for what seemed an immense distance, before he struck bottom. Lying half stunned in a shallow, fetid pool, he heard the funereal thud of the heavy slab as it slid back into place far above him.

6. The Vaults of Ylourgne

Gaspard was revived, after a while, by the chillness of the water in which he lay. His garments were half soaked; and the slimy mephitic pool, as he discovered by his first movement, was within an inch of his mouth. He could hear a steady, monotonous dripping somewhere in the rayless night of his dungeon. He staggered to his feet, finding that his bones were still intact, and began a cautious exploration, Foul drops fell upon his hair and lifted face as he moved; his feet slipped and splashed in the rotten water; there were angry, vehement hissings, and serpentine coils slithered coldly across his ankles.

He soon came to a rough wall of stone, and following the wall with his finger-tips, he tried to determine the extent of the oubliette. The place was more or less circular, without corners, and he failed to form any just idea of its circuit. Somewhere in his wanderings, he found a shelving pile of rubble that rose above the water against the wall; and here, for the sake of comparative dryness and comfort, he ensconced himself, after dispossessimg a number of outraged reptiles. These creatures, it seemed, were inoffensive, and probably belonged to some species of watersnake; but he shivered at the touch of their clammy scales.

Sitting on the rubble-heap, Gaspard reviewed in his mind the various horrors of a situation that was infinitely dismal and desperate. He had learned the incredible, soul-shaking secret of Ylourgne, the unimaginably monstrous and blasphemous project of Nathaire; but now, immured in this noisome hole as in a subterranean tomb, in depths beneath the devil-haunted pile, he could not even warn the world of imminent menace.

The wallet of food, now more than half empty, with which he had started from Vyones, was still hanging at his back; and he assured himself by investigation that his captors had not troubled to deprive him of his dagger. Gnawing a crust of stale bread in the darkness, and caressing with his hand the hilt of the precious weapon, he sought for some rift in the all-environing despair.

He had no means of measuring the black hours that went over him with the slowness of a slime-clogged river, crawling in blind silence to a subterrene sea. The ceaseless drip of water, probably from sunken hill-springs that had supplied the castle in former years alone broke the stillness; but the sound became in time an equivocal monotone that suggested to his half-delirious mind the mirthless and perpetual chuckling of unseen imps. At last, from sheer bodily exhaustion, he fell into troubled nightmare-ridden chamber.

He could not tell if it were night or noon in the world without when he awakened; for the same stagnant darkness, unrelieved by ray or glimmer, brimmed the oubliette. Shivering, he became aware of a steady draught that blew upon him: a dank, unwholesome air, like the breath of unsunned vaults that had wakened into cryptic life and activity during his sleep. He had not noticed the draught heretofore; and his numb brain was startled into sudden hope by the intimation which it conveyed. Obviously there was some underground rift or channel through which the air entered; and this rift might somehow prove to be a place of egress from the oubliette.

Getting to his feet, he groped uncertainly forward in the direction of the draught. He stumbled over something that cracked and broke beneath his heels, and narrowly checked himself from falling on his face in tbe slimy, serpent-haunted pool. Before he could investigate the obstruction or resume his blind groping, he heard a harsh, grating noise above, and a wavering shaft of yellow light came down through the oubliette's opened mouth. Dazzled, he looked up, and saw the round hole ten or twelve feet overhead, through which a dark hand had reached down with a flaring torch. A small basket, containing a loaf of coarse bread and a bottle of wine, was being lowered at the end of a cord.

Gaspard took the bread and wine, and the basket was drawn up. Before the withdrawal of the torch and the re-depositing of the slab, he contrived to make a hasty survey of his dungeon. The place was roughly circular, as he had surmised, and was perhaps fifteen feet in diameter. The thing over which he had stumbled was a human skeleton, lying half on the rubble-heap, half in the filthy water. It was brown and rotten with age, and its garments had long melted away in patches of liquid mould.

The walls were guttered and runnelled by centuries of ooze and their very stone, it seemed, was rotting slowly to decay. In the opposite side, at the bottom, he saw the opening he had, suspected: a low mouth, not much bigger than a foxes' hole, into which the sluggish water fiowed. His heart sank at the sight; for, even if the water were deeper than it seemed, the hole was far too strait for the passage of a man's body. In a state of hopelessness that was like a veritable suffocation, he found his way back to the rubble-pile when the light had been withdrawn.

The loaf of bread and the bottle of wine were still in his hands. Mechanically, with dull, sodden hunger, he munched and drank. Afterwards he felt stronger; and the sour, common wine served to warm him and perhaps helped to inspire him with the idea which he presently conceived.

Finishing the bottle, he found his way across the dungeon to the low, burrow-like hole. The entering air current had strengthened, and this he took for a good omen, Drawing his dagger, he started to pick with the point at the half-rotten, decomposing wall, in an effort to enlarge the opening. He was forced to kneel in noisome silt; and the writhing coils of water-snakes, hissing frightfully, crawled across his legs as he worked. Evidently the hole was their means of ingress and egress, to and from the oubliette.

The stone crumbled readily beneath his dagger, and Gaspard forgot the horror and ghastliness of his situation in the hope of escape. He had no means of knowing the thickness of the wall; or the nature and extent of the subterrenes that lay beyond; but he felt sure that there was some channel of connection with the outer air.

For hours or days, it seemed, he toiled with his dagger, digging blindly at the soft wall and removing the dèbris that splashed in the water beside him. After a while, prone on his belly, he crept into the hole he had enlarged; and burrowing like some laborious mole, he made his way onwards inch by inch.

At last, to his prodigious relief, the dagger-point went through into empty space. He broke away with his hands the thin shell of obstructing stone that remained; then, crawling on in the darkness, he found that he could stand upright on a sort of shelving floor.

Straightening his cramped limbs, he moved on very cautiously. He was in a narrow vault or tunnel, whose sides he could touch simultaneously with his outstretched finger-tips. The floor was a downwards incline; and the water deepened, rising to his knees and then to his waist, Probably the place had once been used as an underground exit from the castle; and the roof, falling in, had dammed the water.

More than a little dismayed, Gaspard began to wonder if he had exchanged the foul, skeleton-haunted oubliette for something even worse. The night around and before him was still untouched by any ray, and the air-current, though strong, was laden with dankness and mouldiness as of interminable vaults.

Touching the tunnel-sides at intervals as he plunged hesitantly into the deepening water, he found a sharp angle, giving upon free space at his right. The space proved to be the mouth of an inter-secting passage, whose flooded bottom was at least level and went no deeper into the stagnant foulness, Exploring it, he stumbled over the beginning of a flight of upward steps. Mounting these through the shoaling water, he soon found himself on dry stone.

The stairs, narrow, broken, irregular, without landings, appeared to wind in some eternal spiral that was coiled lightlessly about the bowels of Ylourgne. They were close and stifling as a tomb, and plainly they were not the source of the air-current which Gaspard had started to follow. Whither they would lead he knew not; nor could he tell if they were the same stairs by which he had been conducted to his dungeon. But he climbed steadily, pausing only at long intervals to regain his breath as best he could in the dead, mephitis-burdened air.

At length, in the solid darkness, far above, he began to hear a mysterious, muffled sound: a dull but recurrent crash as of mighty blocks and masses of falling stone. The sound was unspeakably ominous and dismal, and it seemed to shake the unfathomable walls around Gaspard, and to thrill with a sinister vibration in the steps on which he trod,

He climbed now with redoubled caution and alertness, stopping ever and anon to listen. The recurrent crashing noise grew louder, more ominous, as if it were immediately above; and the listener crouched on the dark stairs for a time that might have been many minutes, without daring to go farther. At last, with disconcerting suddenness, the sound came to an end, leaving a strained and fearful stillness.

With many baleful conjectures, not knowing what fresh enormity he should find, Gaspard ventured to resume his climbing. Again, in the blank and solid stillness, he was met by a sound: the dim, reverberant chanting of voices, as in some Satanic mass or liturgy with dirge-like cadences that turned to intolerably soaring paeans of evil triumph. Long before he could recognize the words, he shivered at the strong, malefic throbbing of the measured rhythm, whose fall and rise appeared somehow to correspond to the heartbeats of some colossal demon.

The stairs turned, for the hundredth time in their tortuous spiral; and coming forth from that long midnight, Gaspard blinked in the wan glimmering that streamed towards him from above. The choral voices met him in a more sonorous burst of infernal sound, and he knew the words for those of a rare and potent incantation, used by sorcerers for a supremely foul, supremely maleficent purpose. Affrightedly, as he climbed the last steps, he knew the thing that was taking place amid the ruins of Ylourgne.

Lifting his head warily above the castle floor, he saw that the stairs ended in a far corner of the vast room in which he had beheld Nathaire's unthinkable creation. The whole extent of the internally dismantled building lay before him, filled with a weird glare in which the beams of the slightly gibbous moon were mingled with the ruddy flames of dying athanors and the coiling, multi-coloured tongues that rose from necromantic braziers.

Gaspard, for an instant, was puzzled by the flood of full moonlight amid the ruins. Then he saw that almost the whole inner wall of the castle, giving on the courtyard, had been removed. It was the tearing-down of the prodigious blocks, no doubt through an extra-human labour levied by sorcery, that he had heard during his ascent from the subterrene vaults. His blood curdled, he felt an actual horripilation, as he realized the purpose for which the wall had been demolished.

It was evident that a whole day and part of another night had gone by since his immurement; for the moon rode high in the pale sapphire welkin. Bathed in its chilly glare, the huge vats no longer emitted their eerie and electric phosphorescence. The couch of Saracen fabrics, on which Gaspard had beheld the dying dwarf, was now half hidden from view by the mounting fumes of braziers and thuribles, amid which the sorcerer's ten pupils, clad in sable and scarlet, were performing their hideous and repugnant rite, with its malefically measured litany.

Fearfully, as one who confronts an apparition reared up from nether hell, Gaspard beheld the colossus that lay inert as if in Cyclopean sleep on the castle flags. The thing was no longer a skeleton: the limbs were rounded into bossed, enormous thews, like the limbs of Biblical giants; the flanks were like an insuperable wall; the deltoids of the mighty chest were broad as platform; the hands could have crushed the bodies of men like millstones.... But the face of the stupendous monster, seen in profile athwart the pouring moon, was the face of the Satanic dwarf, Nathaire — re-magnified a hundred times, but the same in its implacable madness and malevolence!

The vast bosom seemed to rise and fall; and during a pause of the necromantic ritual, Gaspard heard the unmistakable sound of a mighty respiration, The eye in the profile was closed; but its lid appeared to tremble like a great curtain, as if the monster were about to wake; and the outflung hand, with fingers pale and bluish as a row of corpses, twitched unquietly on the castle flags.

An insupportable terror seized the watcher; but even this terror could not induce him to return to the noisome vaults he had left. With infinite hesitation and trepidation, he stole forth from the corner, keeping in a zone of ebon shadow that flanked the castle wall.

As he went, he saw for a moment, through bellying folds of vapour, the couch on which the shrunken form of Nathaire was lying pallid and motionless. It seemed that the dwarf was dead, or had fallen into a stupor preceding death. Then the choral voices, crying their dreadful incantation, rose higher in Satanic triumph; the vapours eddied like a hell-born cloud, coiling about the sorcerers in python-shaped volumes, and hiding again the Orient couch and its corpse-like occupant.

A thraldom of measureless evil oppressed the air. Gaspard felt that the awful transmigration, evoked and implored with ever-swelling, liturgic blasphemies, was about to take place — had perhaps already occurred. He thought that the breathing giant stirred, like one who tosses in light slumber.

Soon the towering, massively recumbent hulk was interposed between Gaspard and the chanting necromancers. They had not seen him; and he now dared to run swiftly, and gained the courtyard unpursued and unchallenged. Thence, without looking back, he fled like a devil-hunted thing upon the steep and chasm-riven slopes below Ylourgne.

7. The Coming of the Colossus

After the cessation of the exodus of liches, a universal terror still prevailed; a wide-flung shadow of apprehension, infernal and funereal, lay stagnantly on Averoigne. There were strange and disastrous portents in the aspect of the skies: flame-bearded meteors had been seen to fall beyond the eastern hills; a comet far in the south had swept the stars with its luminous bosom for a few nights, and had then faded, leaving among men the prophecy of bale and pestilence to come. By day the air was oppressed and sultry, and the blue heavens were heated as if by whitish fires. Clouds of thunder, darkling and withdrawn, shook their fulgurant lances on the far horizons, like some beleaguering Titan army. A murrain, such as would come from the working of wizard spells, was abroad among the cattle. All these signs and prodigies were an added heaviness on the burdened spirits of men, who went to and fro in daily fear of the hidden preparations and machinations of hell.

But, until the actual breaking-forth of the incubated menace, there was no one, save Gaspard du Nord, who had knowledge of its veritable form. And Gaspard, fleeing headlong beneath the gibbous moon towards Vyones, and fearing to hear the tread of a colossal pursuer at any moment, had thought it more than useless to give warning in such towns and villages as lay upon his line of sight. Where, indeed — even if warned — could men hope to hide themselves from the awful thing, begotten by Hell on the ravished charnel, that would walk forth like the Anakim to visit its roaring wrath on a trampled world?

So, all that night, and throughout the day that followed, Gaspard du Nord, with the dried slime of the oubliette on his briar-shredded raiment, plunged like a madman through the towering woods that were haunted by robbers and were-wolves. The westward-falling moon flickered in his eyes betwixt the gnarled sombre boles as he ran; and the dawn overtook him with the pale shafts of its searching arrows. The noon poured over him its white sultriness, like furnace-heated metal sublimed into light; and the clotted filth that clung to his tatters was again turned into slime by his own sweat. But still he pursued his nightmare-harried way, while a vague, seemingly hopeless plan took form in his mind.

In the interim, several monks of the Cistercian brotherhood, watching the grey wall of Ylourgne at early dawn with their habitual vigilance, were the first, after Gaspard, to behold the monstrous horror created by the necromancers. Their account may have been somewhat tinged by a pious exaggeration; but they swore that the giant rose abruptly, standing more than waist-high above the ruins of the barbican, amid a sudden leaping of long-tongued fires and a swirling of pitchy fumes erupted from Malbolge. The giant's head was level with the high top of the donjon, and his right arm, out-thrust, lay like a bar of stormy cloud athwart the new-risen sun.

The monks fell grovelling to their knees, thinking that the Archfoe himself had come forth, using Ylourgne for his gateway from the Pit. Then, across the mile-wide valley, they heard a thunderous peal of demoniac laughter; and the giant, climbing over the mounded barbican at a single step, began to descend the scarped and craggy hill.

When he drew nearer, bounding from slope to slope, his features were manifestly those of some great devil animated with ire and malice towards the sons of Adam. His hair, in matted locks, streamed behind him like a mass of black pythons; his naked skin was livid and pale and cadaverous, with the skin of the dead; but beneath it, the stupendous thews of a Titan swelled and rippled. The eyes, wide and glaring flamed like lidless cauldrons heated by the fires of the unplumbed Pit.

The rumour of his coming passed like a gale of terror through the Monastery. Many of the Brothers, deeming discretion the better part of religious fervour, hid themselves in the stone-hewn cellars and vaults. Others crouched in their cells, mumbling and shrieking incoherent pleas to all the Saints. Still others, the most courageous, repaired in a body to the chapel and knelt in solemn prayer before the wooden Christ on the great crucifix.

Bernard and Stephane, now somewhat recovered from their grievous beating, alone dared to watch the advance of the giant. Their horror was inexpressibly increased when they began to recognize in the colossal features a magnified likeness to the lineaments of that evil dwarf who had presided over the dark, unhallowed activities of Ylourgne; and the laughter of the colossus, as he came down the valley, was like a tempest-borne echo of the damnable cachinnation that had followed their ignominious flight from the haunted stronghold. To Bernard and Stephane, however, it seemed merely that the dwarf, who was no doubt an actual demon, had chosen to appear in his natural form.

Pausing in the valley-bottom, the giant stood opposite the monastery with his flame-filled eyes on a level with the window from which Bemard and Stephane were peering. He laughed again — an awful laugh, like a subterranean rurnbling — and then, stooping, he picked up a handful of boulders as if they had been pebbles, and proceeded to pelt the monastery. The boulders crashed against the walls, as if hurled from great catapults or mangonels of war; but the stout building held, though shaken grievously.

Then, with both hands, the colossus tore loose an immense rock that was deeply embedded in the hillside; and lifting this rock, he flung it at the stubborn walls. The tremendous mass broke in an entire side of the chapel; and those who had gathered therein were found later, crushed into bloody pulp amid the splinters of their carven Christ.

After that, as if disdaining to palter any further with a prey so insignificant, the colossus turned his back on the little monastery, and like some fiend-born Goliath, went roaring down the valley into Averoigne.

As he departed, Bernard and Stephane, still watching from their window, saw a thing they had not perceived heretofore: a huge basket made of planking, that hung suspended by ropes between the giant's shoulders. In the basket, ten men — the pupils and assistants of Nathaire — were being carried like so many dolls or puppets in a peddler's pack.

Of the subsequent wanderings and depredations of the colossus, a hundred legends were long current throughout Averoigne: tales of an unexampled ghastliness, a wanton diabolism without parallel in all the histories of that demon-pestered land.

The goatherds of the hills below Ylourgne saw him coming, and fled with their nimble-footed flocks to the highest ridges. To these he paid little heed, merely trampling them down like beetles when they could not escape from his path. Following the hillstream that was the source of the river Isoile, he came to the verge of the great forest; and here, it is related, he tore up a towering ancient pine by the roots, and snapping off the mighty boughs with his hands, shaped it into a cudgel which he carried henceforward.

With this cudgel, heavier than a battering-ram, he pounded into shapeless ruin a wayside shrine in the outer woods. A hamlet fell in his way, and he strode through it, beating in the roofs, toppling the walls, and crushing the inhabitants beneath his feet.

To and fro in a mad frenzy of destruction, like a deathdrunken Cyclops, he wandered all that day. Even the fierce beasts of the woodland ran from him in fear. The wolves, in mid-hunt, abandoned their quarry and retired, howling dismally with terror, to their rocky dens. The black, savage hunting-dogs of the forest barons would not face him, and hid whimpering in their kennels.

Men heard his mighty laughter, his stormy bellowing; they saw his approach from a distance of many leagues, and fled or concealed themselves as best they could. The lords of moated castles called in their men-at-arms, drew up their drawbridges and prepared as if for the siege of an army. The peasants hid themselves in caverns, in cellars, in old wells, and even beneath hay-mounds, hoping that he would pass them by unnoticed. The churches were crammed with refugees who sought protection of the Cross, deeming that Satan himself, or one of his chief lieutenants, had risen to harry and lay waste the land.

In a voice like summer thunder, mad maledictions, unthinkable obscenities and blasphemies were uttered ceaselessly by the giant as he went to and fro. Men heard him address the litter of black-clad figures that he carried on his back, in tones of admonishment or demonstration such as a master would use to his pupils. People who had known Nathaire recognized the incredible likeness of the huge features, the similarity of the swollen voice to his. A rumour went abroad that the dwarf sorcerer, through his loathly bond with the Adversary, had been permitted to transfer his hateful soul into this Titanic form; and, bearing his pupils with him, had returned to vent an insatiable ire, a bottomless rancour, on the world that had mocked him for his puny physique and reviled him for his sorcery. The charnel genesis of the monstrous avatar was also rumoured; and, indeed it was said that the colossus had openly proclaimed his identity.

It would be tedious to make explicit mention of all the enormities, all the atrocities, that were ascribed to the marauding giant.... There were people — mostly priests and women, it is told — whom he picked up as they fled, and pulled limb from limb as a child might quarter an insect.... And there were worse things, not to be named in this record....

Many eye-witnesses told how he hunted Pierre, the Lord of La Frênaie, who had gone forth with his dogs and men to chase a noble stag in the nearby forest Overtaking horse and rider, he caught them with one hand, and bearing them aloft as he strode over the tree-tops, he hurled them later against the granite walls of the Chateau of La Frênaie in passing. Then, catching the red stag that Pierre had hunted, he flung it after them; and the huge bloody blotches made by the impact of the bashed bodies remained long on the castle stone, and were never wholly washed away by the autumn rains and the winter snows.

Countless tales were told, also, of the deeds of obscene sacrilege and profanation committed by the colossus: of the wooden Virgin that he flung into the Isoile above Ximes, lashed with human gut to the rotting, mail-clad body of an infamous outlaw; of the wormy corpses that he dug with his hands from unconsecrated graves and hurled into the courtyard of the Benedictine abbey of Perigon; of the Church of Ste. Zenobie, which he buried with its priests and congregation beneath a mountain of ordure made by the gathering of all the dungheaps from neighbouring farms.

8. The Laying of the Colossus

Back and forth, in an irregular, drunken, zigzag course, from end to end and side to side of the harried realm, the giant strode without pause, like an energumen possessed by some implacable fiend of mischief and murder, leaving behind him, as a reaper leaves his swath, an ever-lengthening zone of havoc, of rapine and carnage. And when the sun, blackened by the smoke of burning villages, had set luridly beyond the forest, men still saw him moving in the dusk, and heard still the portentous rumbling of his mad, stormy cachinnation.

Nearing the gates of Vyones at sunset, Gaspard du Nord saw behind him, through gaps in the ancient wood, the far-off head and shoulders of the terrible colossus, who moved along the Isoile, stooping from sight at intervals in some horrid deed.

Though numb with weariness and exhaustion, Gaspard quickened his flight. He did not believe, however, that the monster would try to invade Vyones, the especial object of Nathaire's hatred and malice, before the following day. The evil soul of the sorcerous dwarf, exulting in its almost infinite capacity for harm and destruction, would defer the crowning act of vengeance, and would continue to terrorize, during the night, the outlying villages and rural districts.

In spite of his rags and filth, which rendered him practically unrecognizable and gave him a most disreputable air, Gaspard was admitted without question by the guards at the city gate. Vyones was already thronged with people who had fled to the sanctuary of its stout walls from the adjacent countryside; and no one, not even of the most dubious character, was denied admittance. The walls were lined with archers and pike-bearers, gathered in readiness to dispute the entrance of the giant. Crossbowmen were stationed above the gates, and mangonels were mounted at short intervals along the entire circuit of the ramparts. The city seethed and hummed like an agitated hive.

Hysteria and pandemonium prevailed in the streets. Pale, panic-stricken faces milled everywhere in an aimless stream. Hurrying torches flared dolorously in the twilight that deepened as if with the shadow of impending wings arisen from Erebus. The gloom was clogged with intangible fear, with webs of stifling oppression. Through all this rout of wild disorder and frenzy, Gaspard, like a spent but indomitable swimmer breasting some tide of eternal, viscid nightmare, made his way slowly to his attic lodgings.

Afterwards, he could scarcely remember eating and drinking. Overworn beyond the limit of bodily and spiritual endurance, he threw himself down on his pallet without removing his ooze-stiffened tatters, and slept soddenly till an hour half-way between midnight and dawn.

He awoke with the death-pale beams of the gibbous moon shining upon him through his window; and rising, spent the balance of the night in making certain occult preparations which, he felt, offered the only possibility of coping with the fiendish monster that had been created and animated by Nathaire.

Working feverishly by the light of the westering moon and a single dim taper, Gaspard assembled various ingredients of familiar alchemic use which he possessed, and compounded from these, through a long and somewhat cabalistic process, a dark-grey powder which he had seen employed by Nathaire on numerous occasions. He had reasoned that the colossus, being formed from the bones and flesh of dead men unlawfully raised up, and energized only by the soul of a dead sorcerer, would be subject to the influence of this powder, which Nathaire had used for the laying of resurrected liches. The powder, if cast in the nostrils of such cadavers, would cause them to, return peacefully to their tombs and lie down in a renewed slumber of death.

Gaspard made a considerable quantity of the mixture, arguing that no mere finger-pinch would suffice for the lulling of the gigantic charnel monstrosity. His guttering yellow candle was dimmed by the white dawn as he ended the Latin formula of fearsome verbal invocation from which the compound would derive much of its efficacy. The formula, which called for the cooperation of Alastor and other evil spirits, he used with unwillingness. But he knew that there was no alternative: sorcery could be fought only with sorcery.

Morning came with new terrors to Vyones. Gaspard had felt,

through a sort of intuition, that the vengeful colossus, who was said to have wandered with unhuman tirelessness and diabolic energy all night through Averoigne, would approach the hated city early in the day. His intuition was confirmed; for scarcely had he finished his occult labours when he heard a mounting hubbub in the streets, and above the shrill, dismal clamour of frightened voices, the far-off roaring of the giant.

Gaspard knew that he must lose no time, if he were to post himself in a place of vantage from which he could throw his powder into the nostrils of the hundred-foot colossus. The city walls and even most of the church spires, were not lofty enough for this purpose; and a brief reflection told him that the great cathedral, standing at the core of Vyones, was the one place from whose roof he could front the invader with success. He felt sure that the men-at-arms on the walls could do little to prevent the monster from entering and wreaking his malevolent will. No earthly weapon could injure a being of such bulk and nature; for even a cadaver of normal size, reared up in this fashion, could be shot full of arrows or transfixed by a dozen pikes without retarding its progress.

Hastily he filled a huge leathern pouch with the powder; and carrying the pouch at his belt, he joined the agitated press of pople in the street. Many were fleeing towards the cathedral, to seek the shelter of its august sanctity; and he had only to let himself be borne along by the frenzy-driven stream.

The cathedral nave was packed with worshippers, and solemn masses were being said by priests whose voices faltered at times with inward panic. Unheeded by the wan, despairing throng, Gaspard found a flight of coiling stairs that led tortuously to the gargoyle-warded roof of the high tower.

Here he posted himself, crouching behind the stone figure of a cat-headed griffin. From his vantage he could see, beyond the crowded spires and gables, the approaching giant, whose head and torso loomed above the city walls. A cloud of arrows, visible even at that distance, rose to meet the monster, who apparently did not even pause to pluck them from his hide. Great boulders hurled from mangonels were no more to him than a pelting of gravel; the heavy bolts of arbalests, embedded in his flesh, were mere slivers.

Nothing could stay his advance. The tiny figures of a company of pikemen, who opposed him with out-thrust weapons, swept from the wall above the eastern gate by a single sidelong blow of the seventy-foot pine that he bore for a cudgel. Then, having cleared the wall, the colossus climbed over it into Vyones.

Roaring, chuckling, laughing like a maniacal Cyclops, he strode along the narrow streets between houses that rose only to his waist, trampling without mercy everyone who could not escape in time, and smashing in the roofs with stupendous blows of his bludgeon. With a push of his left hand he broke off the protruding gables, and overturned the church steeples with their bells clanging in dolorous alarm as they went down. A woeful shrieking and wailing of hysteria-laden voices accompanied his passing.

Straight towards the cathedral he came, as Gaspard had calculated, feeling that the high edifice would be made the special butt of his malevolence.

The streets were now emptied of people; but, as if to hunt them out and crush them in their hiding-places, the giant thrust his cudgel like a battering-ram through walls and windows and roofs as he went by. The ruin and havoc that he left was indescribable.

Soon he loomed opposite the cathedral tower on which Gaspard waited behind the gargoyle. His head was level with the tower, and his eyes flamed like wells of burning brimstone as he drew near. His lips were parted over stalactitic fangs in a hateful snarl; and he cried out in a voice like the rumbling of articulate thunder:

"Ho! Ye puling priests and devotees of a powerless God! Come forth and bow to Nathaire the master, before he sweeps you into limbo!"

It was then that Gaspard, with a hardihood beyond comparison, rose from his hiding-place and stood in full view of the raging colossus.

"Draw nearer, Nathaire, if indeed it be you, foul robber of tombs and charnels," he taunted. "Come close, for I would hold speech with you."

A monstrous look of astonishment dimmed the diabolic rage on the colossal features. Peering at Gaspard as if in doubt or incredulity, the giant lowered his lifted cudgel and stepped close to the tower, till his face was only a few feet from the intrepid student. Then, when he had apparently convinced himself of Gaspard's identity, the look of maniacal wrath returned, flooding his eyes with Tartarean fire and twisting his lineaments into a mask of Apollyon-like malignity. His left arm came up in a prodigious arc, with twitching fingers that poised horribly above the head of the youth, casting upon him a vulture-black shadow in the full-risen sun. Gaspard saw the white, startled faces of the necromancer's pupils, peering over his shoulder from their plank-built basket.

"Is it you, Gaspard, my recreant pupil?" the colossus roared stormily. "I thought you were rotting in the oubliette beneath Ylourgne — and now I find you perched atop of this accursed cathedral which I am about to demolish! ... You had been far wiser to remain where I left you, my good Gaspard."

His breath, as he spoke, blew like a charnel-polluted gale on the student. His vast fingers, with blackened nails like shovelblades, hovered in ogreish menace. Gaspard had furtively loosened his leathern pouch that hung at his belt, and had untied its mouth. Now, as the twitching fingers descended towards him, he emptied the contents of the pouch in the giant's face, and the fine powder, mounting in a dark-grey cloud, obscured the snarling lips and palpitating nostrils from his view.

Anxiously he watched the effect, fearing that the powder might be useless after all, against the superior arts and Satanical resources of Nathaire. But miraculously, as it seemed, the evil lambence died in the pit-deep eyes, as the monster inhaled the flying cloud. His lifted hand, narrowly missing the crouching youth in its sweep, fell lifelessly at his side. The anger was erased from the mighty, contorted mask, as if from the face of a dead man; the great cudgel fell with a crash to the empty street; and with drowsy, lurching steps, and listless, hanging arms, the giant turned his back to the cathedral and retraced his way through the devastated city.

He muttered dreamily to himself as he went; and people who heard him swore that the voice was no longer the awful, thunderswollen voice of Nathaire, but the tones and accents of a multitude of men, amid which the voices of certain of the ravished dead were recognizable. And the voice of Nathaire himself, no louder now than in life, was heard at intervals through the manifold mutterings, as if protesting angrily.

Climbing the eastern wall as it had come, the colossus went to and fro for many hours, no longer wreaking a hellish wrath and rancour, but searching, as people thought, for the various tombs and graves from which the hundreds of bodies that composed it had been so foully reft. From charnel to charnel, from cemetery to cemetery it went, through all the land; but there was no grave anywhere in which the dead colossus could lie down.

Then, towards evening, men saw it from afar on the red rim of the sky, digging with its hands in the soft, loamy plain beside the river Isoile. There, in a monstrous and self-made grave, the colossus laid itself down, and did not rise again. The ten pupils of Nathaire, it was believed, unable to descend from their basket, were crushed beneath the mighty body; for none of them was ever seen thereafter.

For many days no one dared to approach the place where the corpse lay uncovered in its self-dug grave. And so the thing rotted prodigiously beneath the summer sun, breeding a mighty stench that wrought pestilence in that portion of Averoigne. And they who ventured to go near in the following autumn, when the stench had lessened greatly, swore that the voice of Nathaire, still protesting angrily, was heard by them to issue from the enormous, rook-haunted bulk.

Of Gaspard du Nord, who had been the saviour of the province, it was related that he lived in much honour to a ripe age, being the one sorcerer of that region who at no time incurred the disapprobation of the Church.